# Eyes of Darkness

# Eyes of Darkness

*A Novel*

## JAMAKE HIGHWATER

Lothrop, Lee & Shepard Books • New York

Printed in the United States of America.
*First Edition*

1 2 3 4 5 6 7 8 9 10

*Designed by Sheila Lynch*

Library of Congress Cataloging in Publication Data
Highwater, Jamake.
Eyes of darkness.
Summary: A Santee Sioux Indian named Yesa, after being
taken at age sixteen to live among white men,
becomes a doctor and then returns to the reservation to
live as an Indian.
1. Santee Indians—Juvenile fiction.   2. Indians of
North America—Juvenile fiction. [1. Santee Indians—
Fiction.   2. Indians of North America—Fiction]
I. Title.
PZ7.H5443Ey   1985 [Fic]   82–187
ISBN 0-688-41993-3

Excerpt from *Black Elk Speaks: Being the Life Story of a Holy Man of the Oglala
Sioux* by John G. Neihardt. Copyright 1932, 1959 by John Neihardt.
Published by Simon & Schuster Pocket Books and the University of
Nebraska Press. Used by permission.

# CONTENTS

†
## Part Five
## In the Land of the Dead

†
## Part Six
## In Search of the Real

†
## Part Seven
## The Darkness in Men's Eyes

"Now I can see it all as from a lonely hilltop. I know it was the story of a mighty vision given to a man too weak to use it; of a holy tree that should have flourished in a people's heart with flowers and singing birds, and now is withered; and of a people's dream that died in bloody snow. But the vision was true and mighty, as I know it is true and mighty yet; for such things are of the spirit, and it is in the darkness of their eyes that men get lost."

John Neihardt, *Black Elk Speaks*

*Eyes of Darkness* is a work of fiction, but its historical perspective is derived from the life and works of Charles Alexander Eastman. To all such sources I offer my acknowledgments.     J.H.

For PHYLLIS OLD DOG CROSS
A bridge over troubled water

# Part One

# In the Shadow
# of the Sacred Tree

# RED BIRD

Alexander East was startled as he sat at his desk staring down at his diploma. It was very late and he could not imagine who could be banging at his door.

When he opened it he saw Blue Horse and his wife standing uneasily on his step.

"Much important business, Dr. East. We apologize. We very much apologize for the late hour, but we must talk to you," Blue Horse murmured urgently.

Scarcely had his guests come inside and been seated, when there was another knock at the door. Captain Sword of the Indian police hurried in, followed by Lieutenant Thunder Deer and almost all the other reservation policemen.

Alexander was growing anxious to learn the reason for this midnight meeting, but custom required him first to greet each person, hand them some tobacco, and then wait in silence for everyone to smoke in a ceremonial expression of tribal unity.

After a long silence, Chief Blue Horse finally got up and shook Alexander's hand. Then he began to speak. He explained that he greatly needed the advice of Dr. Alexander East, for a dangerous situation confronted the people of the reservation.

"I don't understand," Alexander said as he gazed at the solemn faces of his tribespeople.

Captain Sword, the leader of the Indian police force for the reservation, stood up. "I must tell you, Doctor East," he said in a whisper, "that we are going to have much trouble. I must tell you that a new religion has been proclaimed by many Indians who live in the Rocky Mountains."

"It is true," the chief said with growing excitement. "Not long ago great Sitting Bull sent some of his best men to talk to the leaders of this new religion. And when they returned they said they had seen the prophet. That is the news given to Sitting Bull."

"But who is this Indian prophet?" Alexander asked.

"He is called Wovoka and his followers are many," Captain Sword intoned.

"They profess that if Indians follow Wovoka he will cause the earth to shake, destroying all the towns of the white men. Then famine and pestilence will drive them back into the sea. That is what the prophet has promised," the chief explained.

"That is true," the captain murmured cautiously, gazing intently at Alexander. "It is said that all Indians who fast and pray and perform the holy dance will live and prosper when the white men are driven away."

"But surely, my good friends, you cannot believe this!" Alexander exclaimed.

No one spoke.

Alexander sighed with dismay.

Finally Captain Sword spoke, "You are new to us. You have been at the schools of the white man. You have learned his language and you have become a good doctor. But you have been away from your people for a very long time, Doctor East. You do not understand us anymore. . . ."

Just as Alexander was about to object, Chief Blue Horse politely interrupted. "My friend, do not be angry at Captain Sword's words. We have welcomed you here. In the good days you have lived with us. The people have come to respect your medicine. Now we face a dangerous situation, and we have come to you for advice. Our reservation has been free from this new religion until now. But we have begun to see the shirts and dresses painted with Moons and Stars. These are the costumes of the Ghost Dance, as it is called by the prophet. That is how we know this new religion has come to us. The Indian agent tells us that the Father in Washington wishes the Ghost Dance stopped. But I know that our people will not stop and so I am troubled, my friend. I fear that again there will be uprisings, and that many of our people will die."

Alexander listened in silence, taken completely by surprise. While at school in the East he had heard nothing of uprisings or of a new religion. Captain Sword and Chief Blue Horse gave Alexander long, intense looks, awaiting his response. The wind wailed along the timbers. The tin roof of the dispensary rattled noisily.

"Ai . . ." Alexander said with a troubled expression, "how difficult this is for us. Yet there can be only one thing for us to do. We must try to use every means we can to bring about a peaceful solution. We must try to reason with these hotheads, even if they call us traitors. They are our brothers and sisters and surely they will listen to us."

"They will not listen," Captain Sword said. "My police have tried to be patient with the Ghost Dancers, but they will not listen. And they do not think of us as their brothers. They claim that we have given our hearts to the white men and they consider us enemies."

Alexander felt an intense sadness sweep over him.

"You have not lived among us for many years," Blue Horse said. "You do not understand that life on the reservation has changed us. We are no longer the same people, Doctor."

Before Alexander could respond there came another urgent

knock at his door. This time it was a clerk summoning the doctor to an emergency meeting in the office of the agent in charge of the reservation. Quickly, Alexander nodded a farewell to his visitors and quietly closed the door behind him.

When he entered the agent's office, he sensed the same atmosphere that he had felt among the Indians who had assembled in his dispensary, except none of these people were Indian. The agent and his chief clerk, a visiting inspector from the government, and several other white men whom Alexander did not recognize eyed him warily. The only woman present was Miss Elaina Goode, a handsome lady charged with the religious training of the reservation children.

Dr. East nodded formally while the agent began speaking in a calculatedly calm voice. "You see, Doctor," the agent was saying with a thin smile of confidence on his lips, "there has been a bit of trouble . . . certain hostilities . . . small and scattered but, we fear, nonetheless hostilities . . . organized and planned with remarkable skill. Even the Indian police were taken entirely by surprise, and no one knows quite what to do. There has been no loss of life, but it seems to be only a matter of time before these little scrimmages will encourage a full-scale uprising by the fanatics in the tribe."

Alexander looked at the worried faces all around him.

"But surely," he said, "you don't believe that any of us would harm you! We are your friends!"

No one responded. Alexander looked at each person in turn. All but Miss Goode turned away self-consciously.

"In any event, Doctor," the agent continued in a formal, polite voice, "we must be prepared. And I shall be glad to have your views on this matter."

A stream of distressing questions flowed through Alexander's mind. Why were no other Indians invited to this meeting? Why weren't the chief and the captain of the Indian police, the elders, the devout Christians among the tribe invited to express their views on the situation?

"Gentlemen . . . Miss Goode . . ." Alexander said, with some difficulty, "I must tell you frankly that I am distressed by your panic and by your suspicion of your Indian friends. I must assure you that there is no plot against you. There is no wish among the elders to make war upon anyone. And certainly not upon our white friends."

"Doctor East," the government inspector said, with a gesture of his hand that dismissed all that Alexander had said, "there have been unfortunate incidents!" Then he turned away from Alexander and continued: "I must tell you once again, gentlemen, it would be utter madness not to call in the troops at once."

"The troops!" Alexander exclaimed. "Certainly you are not thinking of calling for the military!"

Silence filled the room.

"If you bring in the troops," Alexander said in a low, urgent voice, "the Ghost Dancers will see them as a challenge. They will be put on the defensive. Their pride will not tolerate a show of military power."

"Doctor East," the agent said, "I had counted on your being a bit more sympathetic to our views. We cannot be concerned in this situation with the pride of a bunch of renegades and fanatics. It is our first duty to safeguard the lives and property of the government and its employees. And it is my very considered opinion that we can best do this by calling for soldiers without the slightest delay. I have sent for you in the hope that you might approve of my plan. Your own life wouldn't be worth a thing if these hotheads come riding in here with their rifles. As far as they are concerned you are not an Indian anymore, Doctor East."

"I don't believe that!" Alexander exclaimed. "I simply do not believe that—"

But the agent interrupted. "It is settled! We will send for the military without additional delay."

Early in the morning a few days later, Alexander was awakened by Blue Horse shouting, "Come quick! Soldiers are on their way. They'll be here within the hour!"

Alexander tumbled out of bed and pulled his trousers and shirt over his nightclothes. He peered out the window, looking toward the little railroad town in the distance. A cloud of dust moved toward the agency, marking the march of the Ninth Cavalry. As he watched, panic began to break out in the camp. Women and children, fearing the soldiers might attack any Indian they encountered, came running into the agency office for refuge. Men who hadn't heard of the impending arrival of the troops rushed to the dispensary, demanding to know what the approach of soldiers meant.

Alexander did what he could to assure them that the military was there only to preserve peace. "We are friends of the white man," he said. "They will not harm their friends." But the suspicions of the old warriors were not allayed. The troops, headed by a Major Whiteside, set up a temporary camp in the open turf in front of the agency buildings. News of their arrival quickly spread the entire length of the reservation. The major had a reputation as an unyielding and stern Indian fighter. Wild and terrifying rumors began to circulate. On every hill Indian scouts closely watched the white soldiers.

"We must ask you, Doctor," a young cavalry officer stated politely, "not to leave your quarters until this situation has been cleared up." Alexander stared thoughtfully out his office window at a little red bird drumming frantically at the pane.

"Am I to understand that I am under house arrest simply because I am an Indian?"

"It is entirely for your own protection, Doctor. Some of the renegades have made threats against your life."

Before Alexander could reply the soldier left, closing the door behind him. Alexander continued to watch the little red bird. He was reminded of his grandmother and the days that were lost in the deluge of time. He remembered the look of deep concern on her face when she had learned he was going away to the "white man's" school.

Alexander's thoughts were interrupted by a frantic banging at the door. A young Indian runner burst into the room. "Captain Sword has sent me!" the boy exclaimed. "I bring terrible news!" He sank to the floor, exhausted by the emotional burden of his words.

"I have been sent to warn everyone here." He paused, trembling. "Sitting Bull is dead." Upon close questioning by Alexander, the young Indian went on to tell how, at Fort Yates, some two hundred miles north, Sitting Bull had been killed by Indian police while resisting arrest. A number of his most loyal braves and several policemen had been killed also. The remnant of Sitting Bull's band had fled in the direction of the agency. They had been joined by Chief Big Foot from the Cheyenne River Agency.

"They aren't coming here, are they?" Alexander's entire body tensed.

"Yes, yes," the young Indian blurted out as he glanced nervously toward the window.

"What shall we do now?" Alexander whispered, his face turning ashen.

The whole countryside was in a state of panic. United States troops continued to gather at strategic points; border towns

along the reservation fortified themselves; and everywhere there were shouts of fear and rage among those who had long searched for an excuse to attack the reservation Indians.

General Brooke undertook negotiations with the Ghost Dancers, and soon word reached Alexander that the general had induced the members of the religious group to camp near the agency as a demonstration of peace and order.

The Ghost Dancers camped on a wide flatland a mile north of the agency. They took off their ceremonial costumes and hid them. They bowed to the guns of the soldiers and sat silently around their campfires, fearful of the general's eagerness to attack them.

Meanwhile, on orders from the government agent, the boarding school door had closed, locking in hundreds of Indian children. Supposedly, it was for their own safety, but Alexander realized they were really hostages for the good behavior of their warrior fathers.

At the agency all the government employees and their families would no longer venture outside without a military escort. Every white person on the reservation—traders, missionaries, ranchers, army wives, and even newspaper people from the East—squeezed into the protective walls of the agency headquarters. They even gathered in the dispensary, but looked upon Alexander with the greatest caution, as if at any moment he might pull off his clothes and begin a terrifying dance in their midst.

Ironically, the Christmas season was fast approaching, and Father Jutz, a Catholic missionary who was trusted by the Indians, made his way through the camps, trying to encourage holiday spirit. The children of the Sunday school, who were also locked into their quarters, were nonetheless eagerly awaiting the feast days and, with the help of Miss Elaina Goode, were making paper decorations.

Since all branches of the agency had been closed down and the

people were camped in a tight, protective circle around the headquarters, it was decided by Father Jutz to place one large Christmas tree in the chapel and to distribute gifts to a separate congregation each evening. The smiles and generosity of the good Father gradually quelled the anxiety of the people, and a sense of tranquillity descended upon the encampment.

Only three days after Christmas, 1890, the news arrived that Chief Big Foot and his entire band of Ghost Dancers from the Cheyenne River Reservation were quickly approaching the agency. This was the news that everyone had feared, for the word had been received that Major Whiteside had orders from Washington to intercept Big Foot and place him under arrest. If he failed and Big Foot managed to infiltrate the reservation, the troops were instructed to kill not only him but also every other Indian within miles.

Moments after the news of Chief Big Foot's approach was known, Alexander saw the Seventh Cavalry under Colonel Forsythe ride off toward a nearby stream called Wounded Knee Creek. Father Jutz anxiously followed an hour or so later, hoping that he might avert an outbreak of hostilities by talking to the troops and Indians. Alexander intended to ride out with the Father, but Elaina Goode begged him to remain behind at the agency where he might help comfort the terrified Indian children.

The early morning of December 29 was bright and chilly. Vapors rose from the patches of snow in the sunshine. The land was silent, almost as if every creature had fled, aware of a terrible and inevitable catastrophe. Alexander stood at his window, peering toward Wounded Knee and straining his ears to hear the slightest sound.

It was silent. Utterly silent.

Then suddenly in the middle of the morning, he shuddered as

he heard the distant muffled roar of Hotchkiss guns. The sound instantly brought wailing Indians out of their lodges, and soon the women were singing lamentations as the braves gathered and murmured together in foreboding. They had thought the days of war were over. They no longer had a taste for battle, and had grown stiff and unpracticed from life on the reservation.

Helpless and alone, they listened as the echo of the big guns rumbled over the plains.

Two hours later, a lone rider was seen approaching at full speed. It took him only a few minutes to reach the agency, and after leaping from his exhausted pony, he handed a message to General Brooke's orderly.

Almost at the same moment an Indian messenger came running on foot along the northern ridges, carrying news to his own people.

Big Foot's entire band had been murdered by the soldiers! Now there would surely be a full-scale uprising!

At once a shrill tumult arose from the encampment. The white tipis disappeared as if they had been blown away by the wind. Immediately the caravans of Indians took flight, heading toward the natural fortress of the Badlands, where the people often retreated beyond the reach of soldiers.

The Indians who had sworn loyalty were as frightened as the Ghost Dancers who had come into the agency on a mission of peace. Women and children began to pour into the office, the dispensary, and every other available shelter. They cowered under tables and beds, moaning fearfully.

Elaina Goode at once set to work comforting the refugees and trying to provide tea for them. Alexander paced back and forth, torn between remaining at the agency and running off into the nightmarish labyrinth of the Badlands.

While Alexander tried to reach a decision, sentinels began taking up positions at every door of the agency. Machine guns were trained on the silent, empty flatlands surrounding the little ramshackle cluster of unbarricaded buildings.

Still Alexander did not know what to do, whether to stay at his hospital or to join his own people in their flight. But before he could decide, some hotheaded braves fired on the sentinels and wounded two of them. Alexander's decision was abruptly made for him, and he hurried to the aid of the injured men.

Suddenly, the Indian police who had remained loyal to Captain Sword began to shoot back at the braves, who were trying to set fire to some of the outlying buildings.

General Brooke ran out into the open, shouting at the top of his voice to the Indian police. "Stop! Stop!" he was yelling over the gunfire. "Doctor East, tell those men in there to stop firing!"

Bullets whistled through the air as Alexander rushed to urge the over-zealous policemen to listen to the General's orders. The scattered barrage of shots ceased as the rebellious braves slipped away. They had not succeeded in burning any of the buildings, and for the moment there was an uneasy truce.

The dispensary was now full of muttering and weeping refugees. Their eyes were so full of fear that Alexander could not look at them. In the old days there had been spirit and hope among his people, even in the midst of the most fearsome battles. He could recall the strength in the face of Uncheedah and the pride in the eyes of Mysterious Medicine. But now the people were helpless—without guns to protect themselves or horses upon which to escape. They huddled together miserably and wept.

Alexander called aside Captain Sword and quietly asked him to saddle three horses and to stay by them. "When the fighting begins, my friend" he whispered, "I beg you to take Miss Goode and see that she makes her way safely to the railroad station."

Then Alexander went over to the rectory. He offered the third horse to the wife of the Reverend Cook, but she absolutely refused to leave the agency without her husband. Resolutely he returned to the dispensary, where he was confronted by an equally adamant Miss Goode, who insisted upon staying while there was the slightest chance of her helping the Christian Indians who had crowded into the rectory.

There was nothing more Alexander could do now but wait.

In the evening Alexander stood at his window, gazing toward the place called Wounded Knee, trying to put to rest the ghosts of his people. But he was unable to send the terrible phantoms away until, at last, a small red bird fluttered momentarily against the windowpane, chirping desperately and shaking its feathers in a magical dance.

Alexander took a deep breath as he moved his hand toward the little red bird and, tentatively, made a sound just like the ones he had made as a boy when he used to talk to the animals.

For just a moment the bird seemed to understand. For a moment it hovered against the glass, peering at Alexander, its fiery eyes full of a wisdom so great that it filled him with something he had not felt for many years. The bird lingered only a moment and then burst into flight.

"You must not give up," Elaina whispered as she stepped into the dispensary. "There are hundreds of good people who still believe in you, Doctor East."

Alexander laughed dryly. The hundreds of people who believed in him did not live on Indian reservations. They did not hunger for an ancient heritage that had been taken away from them. And they did not know the endless rage that now filled him.

"You must try," Miss Goode was saying. "You must try to believe that some of us care."

Alexander shook his head and smiled with bitterness. There was no possibility, none whatever, for an Indian to be heard or believed. Unless he spoke like a white man and dressed like a white man and acted like a white man . . . and prayed and dreamed and ate and slept and breathed like a white man . . . there was no chance for his voice to be heard.

He stood there silently without looking at Elaina Goode. He didn't want to look at her. He wanted to be alone, to turn slowly around and around to try to find the center of his life. But he could not find it. Everything had gone wrong. His Indian friends no longer believed in him. They kept their distance, for to them, he was just another white man who had made promises he could not keep. They wanted no part of Alexander East.

Now there was a knock at the door and Elaina opened it with expectation. An old man stood on the steps. It was Chief Blue Horse.

He entered humbly, his rain-soaked hat in his hands, mumbling a shy greeting to Elaina Goode, and then stood silently while he watched Dr. East.

Alexander did not want to look at Blue Horse. He was still a chief, yet his own people no longer respected him. The white men treated him like a child, giving him sweets in return for his mark on the documents they put before him. Alexander could not look at Blue Horse because he was afraid that he might see a reflection of his own pain and confusion in the chief's eyes. Soon the old man winced with shame and went away, stumbling out the door as Miss Goode tried to assure him that Dr. East was not feeling well.

Alexander began slowly turning around in the dark dispensary, trying to find his balance, twisting his fingers together in a terrible rage. A terrible fear. He gazed toward the window, searching for the little red bird that had escaped into the sky.

"Doctor East . . ." Elaina Goode whispered, and tried to touch Alexander's shoulder. He withdrew at once and stood at a great distance from her. Suddenly he began to tremble and stagger toward the window, gasping for air. The feeling that he would die from his immense sorrow, rage, and pain overwhelmed him.

He uttered a piercing shout and frantically reached into the air for the red bird. With a shattering crash, his hand burst through the windowpane and blood poured from his fingers.

"Oh my God!" Elaina Goode shouted as she rushed to help him.

He pushed her away with such force that she struck the wall and fell to the floor, where she stared at him in sudden fear.

"Now," Alexander said in a whisper, as he methodically, washed and dressed his wounds. ". . . Now you are thinking that I am a savage like all the rest."

Then he laughed and slouched into a chair. The rage, the sorrow, the madness had passed.

"I cannot stay here anymore," he said, without looking at Miss Goode.

It was getting dark and from somewhere in the distance came the small voice of a bird.

"It doesn't matter why. . . . I just cannot stay here anymore. I have got to get away," he muttered as he stared down at his bandaged hand. "If I stay here any longer, all that will be left of me will be neckties and buttons. Just buttons and pretty neckties. That is all that will be left."

Miss Goode arose cautiously and slowly made her way toward the door.

Alexander ignored her. He was turning around and around. "If I remain here," he said, standing and staring anxiously in one direction and then in another, "if I remain, if I continue to try to do whatever it is that I am supposed to be doing here, then I don't know what will become of me. If I do not follow the path that was given to me long ago I will become something empty and false. I will become a useless old man like Blue Horse. And so, do you see, Miss Goode, I must not stay here any longer."

Looking at him with an expression of confusion and pain on her handsome face, Miss Goode was unable to speak. Abruptly she stepped back, standing very tall as though to steel herself for whatever might come next. But she could not restrain the tears that flooded her eyes. She shook her head and murmured something she herself could not understand. Then she quickly turned and ran out the door.

"Oh my God . . ." Alexander moaned helplessly, turning around and around, trying to find the beginning, trying to find the place where his life had begun. "How did I get here and how is it that I have changed?" he asked the dark room. "How is it that I have changed so utterly?" he exclaimed again and again as he stared toward the broken window, through which a wisp of icy air made its way, carrying with it fragile memories of a small red bird.

Part Two

# In the Springtime
# of the Sacred Tree

# HAKADAH, THE PITIFUL LAST

I n the good days, before the bird had escaped into the sky, the world was golden. The air was blue and the earth was green and each thing rested upon the other. The holy tree flourished, and in its leafy shadow all things lived in peace. In the deep forest leaves fell slowly and each evening was filled with many songs. Everywhere, the tall grass twisted sweet and tender across endless prairies.

It was during one of these evenings that the voice of a newborn child called out, gasping for the breath of life. The mighty wind entered the child's body, but his poor mother was dangerously ill. The medicine man crouched beside her and murmured, "The child will be a holy man, but the mother will die."

And so it was that Alexander East came into the world.

A terrible silence filled the lodge where he was born.

"Ah . . ." the medicine man chanted sorrowfully, "like all newborn males, this boy must wait until he shall earn a dignified name. Until that day he will be called Hakadah, 'the pitiful last,' because he is the youngest of four children whose handsome young mother is soon to die."

The people wept as they withdrew from the dark lodge. They shook their heads and gazed at the beautiful mother, who gasped as she embraced her infant. "Pity me," she whispered to her mother-in-law. "Stay and listen to what I tell you."

The old woman knelt by her daughter-in-law and wiped the tears from her cheeks.

"Listen," the dying woman muttered. ". . . I give you this child for your very own. I cannot trust my mother with him, for she is vain and stingy and she will neglect him, and he will surely die."

"But there will be trouble if I try to take him from her," the old woman said.

"Please, listen to what I ask of you. Take this newborn child! Tell me that you promise to make him your own! Do you promise to do this for me?"

"Yes . . . yes . . ." the old woman sighed.

No sooner had she spoken these words than the young mother's face turned gray and the light went out in her black eyes. Her arms became limp, and little Hakadah whimpered.

The old woman, with tears in her eyes, stepped out of the lodge and spoke to the relatives gathered outside. "I take this child as my own," she said. "I shall keep him until he dies, and then I shall put him in his mother's grave."

The old woman did not wait for a reply. She moved to carry the child away. And when someone objected, she stopped abruptly and raised her hand as a look of immense power flooded her ancient face. For a moment she stood her ground, gazing silently at the relatives of the dead woman, and then she nodded and continued on her way. No one spoke again as they watched her carry the child into her tipi.

Uncheedah was a woman of great character and spirit. She had lived through many difficult years, and the pain of living lingered in her proud face. She was not the kind of person who took a promise lightly. And, though old and poor, she was determined to give little Hakadah all the love and attention she had given to her own firstborn, the boy's father, Many Lightnings.

Uncheedah made the child garments of the softest skins. She bathed him and rubbed oil into his long black hair. And if he awakened in the night, she sang to him in her marvelous, deep voice.

She never left the child alone. When the women went to the forest to cut wood, she carried Hakadah with her, securely wrapped in his cradleboard. And while she worked, she suspended him from a bough so that the slightest breeze would gently swing his cradle.

It was there in the silent forest that she began to notice that whenever she left the child the birds and squirrels fearlessly flocked around him, chirping and singing loudly. If she approached her grandson, the animals unwillingly fled from the delighted boy, who seemed to understand the conversations of the animals. As soon as Uncheedah went back to her work, the animals would return, surrounding Hakadah and twittering earnestly while the child answered them in his own mysterious dialect.

"Hakadah!" the grandmother exclaimed. "You are truly a holy person! Listen, my child . . . listen to *Sheckoka*—the robin —for you must learn his voice.

"Do you hear *Oopehanska*—the thrush?

"Hush, Hakadah! Do you hear the cry of *Hinakaga*—the owl? He is watching from the treetops!"

And so, Grandmother Uncheedah taught Hakadah the voices of nature. She named the plants and herbs for him. And she helped him find his way through the deep shadows of the sacred tree.

Then one day the boy's father, Many Lightnings, burst into the lodge, shouting that everyone must run away and hide for there was going to be a great battle with the white soldiers!

Uncheedah grabbed the child and hurried with him into the forest. The men dressed in their most splendid regalia and began singing strong songs to rouse their courage.

The people of the tribe had been awaiting the distribution of their government annuity—that payment of money, goods, and food given them as compensation for the loss of their homeland. But the annuity had not arrived. The people had already waited so long that they had missed their annual migration to Dakota Territory to hunt buffalo. And now they found themselves hungry and forsaken—without game and without the money and food the white men had promised.

A small band of young braves had become consumed with rage and had killed five white people, exposing the entire tribe to the vengeance of angry soldiers. Now, Chiefs Little Crow and Shakopee had little choice but to call upon their warriors. And so the Minnesota Indians went to battle.

# ESCAPE

**M**any Lightnings called out repeatedly, searching among the trees until he found Uncheedah hovering protectively over Hakadah.

"Come quickly," the father said. "We have taken yokes of oxen and big lumber wagons from farmers killed in the battle. You must pack at once. We must escape to British Columbia! Many white men were killed! Quickly, Mother! Don't waste a moment! The soldiers will attack by morning!"

The old woman whispered anxiously as she hurried back to the camp and began to take down the tipi.

"Do as your grandmother tells you!" Many Lightnings told his youngest son. "You are the pitiful last—but still you must honor your poor mother's memory with courage. No matter what happens, you must listen to Uncheedah. She is my mother and she has given me much wisdom which lives among her many years. Now she will give of herself to you, Hakadah. But to receive you must open your heart and listen carefully to everything she tells you!"

Hakadah nodded solemnly, peering intently into his father's face. Then Many Lightnings touched him gently on the head and turned to the task of hitching the oxen to the wagon.

Hakadah looked with great interest at the peculiar white and gray animals whose wide faces were full of age and knowing. He was delighted that his family would ride behind such wise old creatures, and was anxious to climb into the brightly painted wagon. He had never ridden in a white man's wagon before, and he marveled at its four large round legs that squealed like pigs as they turned! It seemed to Hakadah that the wagon was a living creature and the tug of the somber oxen simply roused it into a life of its own!

By nightfall the women had packed and loaded the family's possessions into the wagon. Many Lightnings assembled his sons and his mother, Uncheedah, and a few of the elders. His brother, Mysterious Medicine, took charge of the little band. The tribe stood silently in the dark, gazing sadly at this good land they were leaving behind. Uncheedah muttered a prayer, blessing the trees and the grass that had given shelter and nourishment to the people and the horses. She thanked the creek and the sky for their friendship and beauty. And then, as the old ones silently wept, the family climbed into the wagon and joined the rest of the refugees. With a single command from Mysterious Medicine, the oxen lurched forward and the familiar Minnesota landscape rolled back into the darkness and vanished.

In the morning, after traveling the entire night without sleep, they found themselves in a strange and ominous land. Exhausted but still fearful of the vengeance of the soldiers, they continued through the wide river valleys, northward toward the Canadian border.

Hakadah's brothers, Chatanna, Noma, and Okha, had become expert at leaping in and out of the moving wagon as the oxen lumbered along in their slow, steady pace. They would shout joyously as they scrambled into the vehicle, and then with arms spread like the wings of a bird they would jump to the ground, staggering to keep their balance.

Finally Hakadah mustered the courage to try the perilous leap himself.

"No, no . . ." Uncheedah exclaimed as she turned to see the child leave the wagon's edge and fall into space. It was too late.

Hakadah had thought his brothers had stepped on the turning wheel to lessen their fall. He soon realized his error. He cautiously placed his moccasined foot on the wheel and before he knew what was happening, he was thrown violently under the wagon. Fortunately, Uncheedah's desperate shouts roused the driver of the wagon traveling directly behind. He quickly pulled his team to a stop, just before it ran over Hakadah, who lay whimpering on the ground—frightened but unhurt.

"Ai!" Uncheedah muttered, brushing him off and staring into his face with a scowl. "We are fleeing for our lives and you and your brothers have nothing better to do than try to kill yourselves! Ai! What foolishness!"

For the rest of the day Hakadah sat sullenly in the wagon, hanging onto the side and whispering every possible reproach to the white man's vehicle. The next morning he climbed onto an Indian travois pulled by a horse, and could not be persuaded to ride in the wagon again. He was truly glad when his father eventually abandoned it beside the Missouri River.

The Missouri was more treacherous than any river in the region. Its swift currents surged into one another and threw up gushers of thick brown water. It was not a river that could be safely crossed. But news came up the valley that General Sibley was in close pursuit. The people had no choice; they had to attempt to ford the river in frail buffalo-skin boats.

"I would rather be killed by this great river than by those soldiers!" Grandmother Uncheedah exclaimed resolutely as she tied up her skirt.

"The *washechu*—the white men—are coming in great numbers with their big guns," Mysterious Medicine called out.

"Most of our young men have remained behind to fight them off so we can gain time to escape with the women and old people," Many Lightnings added solemnly. "But if we do not hurry the soldiers will kill all of us!"

At once the people went to work, making little, round boats of skins that they braced with frail ribs cut from willows. There was much praying and many shouted commands as the people edged out into the swirling brown water. The children wept as they were tied into the little boats. Then the women cautiously swam out into the rapid current, towing two or three boats behind them.

The furious water churned and leaped all around Hakadah as the fragile boat bucked and turned through the powerful waves. Uncheedah swam with strong, long strokes, tugging the little craft into the wide, rushing turbulence of the angry river. The child wanted to cry out, but he clenched his fists and stared across the river and would not make a sound.

The river was in a terrible rage and fought the people trying to move through its powerful currents. The river did not want to let the people pass. No matter how desperately they swam for the shore, it sucked them back into the depths.

Hakadah panted in dread as he watched his grandmother's arms splashing in the water, clutching at the waves, fighting forward with all their strength. Uncheedah cried out in rage as she swam, driven by her promise to protect Hakadah. She summoned all her power and fought with all her might, until at last the river gradually released her from its twisting brown body. Exhausted, she staggered onto the shore and, falling to the ground, gasped for breath.

But there was no time to rest. The shouts of the soldiers could be heard in the distance. Their rifle shots resounded across the wide river, singing a deadly song. The people stumbled and shouted as they pulled the horses and oxen from the water, strapped the children into the saddles or tied them to the old people. In the long night marches to flee the soldiers, they suffered greatly. No one slept or ate for many days. The water supply ran out, and the days and nights were filled with fear and pain.

Now their friendly land was behind them, and the people were compelled to trespass upon the country of their tribal enemies. In every direction there was danger, and only the greatest vigilance saved them.

The hostile Indians watched but they did not attack. Day after day they followed at a distance while the fugitive tribe hurried toward the mountains where they might find shelter. The eyes of the enemies were everywhere. The war whoops echoed all around, and the children were afraid. The women and old men sang rousing songs and chanted stories of ancient victories, which together gave the small ones courage and fired the young men with much daring.

Finally a morning dawned when the people could see the mountains just a day's journey away. The soldiers had fallen far behind, and the angry tribes of the alien land were also gone. At last the starving people were able to make camp and hunt for food and water. That night they ate contentedly around small fires and then slept soundly upon the fragrant grass of autumn.

It was in the darkest night that the horses began to prance and whinny.

Hakadah awakened to the sound, knowing instantly that something was wrong.

"Smoke . . ." the little boy murmured in dread, as he leaped to his feet and rushed to his grandmother's side.

She was fully awake, stumbling in the darkness and calling anxiously to her two sons.

Many Lightnings and his brother, Mysterious Medicine, were

already outside, sounding the alarm. Soon the people tumbled from their lodges and stood horrified as they peered far out across the black prairie, where in the distant night an orange apparition sputtered and leaped into the air.

It was a vast, roaring grass fire!

"Hurry! We must all hurry!" Hakadah's uncle, Mysterious Medicine, shouted in his strong, commanding voice. "We must flee! It is coming this way!"

A great bellow of fear went up from the people as they swarmed over the encampment and, in a fierce calm, hurriedly packed their possessions, saddled the horses, and began their evacuation.

"We must move south as quickly as possible," Mysterious Medicine shouted. "Many Lightnings," he told his brother, "you and your family lead and I will follow behind the last of the old people."

The horses shuddered and stepped wildly as they pressed against the taut reins, shaking their heads. The smell of smoke was everywhere. It spooked the animals, and their great eyes glowed with panic while their nostrils quivered and frothed.

Except for the grunting of the horses and the prancing of their nervous hooves, there was not a single sound in the wide black landscape that spread in every direction.

*Utter stillness!*

The silence surrounded the people. Endless darkness also surrounded them. There was nothing but the wide night, broken by a fragile line of ghastly dancing flames silently glimmering far, far across the vast prairie.

The people blindly rode southward, moving through the great darkness as if they were being led by some knowing spirit. Hakadah and the other children were silent. No one wept or cried out. No one complained or spoke. The band traveled in silence, trying to outrun the great fire that was roaring down upon them.

Now the smoke was getting thick, and the flames were no longer little red figures in the distance. They had grown into a blizzard of giants, leaping and bounding forward in great fiery steps, destroying everything in the path.

"Hurry! Hurry!" Many Lightnings urged the people. Hakadah clung to his grandmother and stared out into the night, where red ogres were changing into gigantic flying birds of flame. The air was filled with them, bursting into crimson flight and setting the night on fire. Hakadah covered his face and tried not to cry. He could not look at the enormous monsters that were making their way toward him across the grassland. He could not look at them anymore!

Now the great wind from the fire came sweeping past the people as they fled. And with the wind came the roar of the flames, resounding across the silent landscape like the rage of a thousand mountain lions. The noise was so great that the people could no longer hear the commands of their leaders.

And all the time the wall of fire came closer.

Hakadah buried his head in his grandmother's arms as the night burst open, exploding into clouds of fire, billowing and rolling across the land toward the desperately running people.

Antelope careened out of the darkness, bounding wildly in front of the horses, dashing headlong, and then vanishing into the night. Their panic lingered as Hakadah watched them dart through the grass, which had turned bright yellow in the blistering light of the fire.

Frightened wolves, yowling and panting, moved swiftly through the undergrowth, with ears back and tails between their legs, racing frantically to escape the fire.

The roar of the flames was deafening, and yet the bellowing of stampeding buffalo could be heard in every direction, terrifying Hakadah lest the huge animals suddenly appear out of the darkness and crush everyone.

Grandmother Uncheedah began to cough. Her eyes burned and she could not breathe. Everyone was strangling on the dense white smoke that swept all around them. Hakadah choked and cried out, and his grandmother covered his head and face with her skin robe.

The great heat swirled in the air, resounding like thunder as it fell upon them. Now the whole flatland was lit up in the dazzling path of the fire. Burning animals, screaming and leaping and falling, came flying out of the wall of flame. Birds fell from the sky like rain as the fire reached up toward them. Cinders and sparks exploded in the air, while thousands of screeching mice sped through the thickets, fleeing under the hooves of the frenzied horses.

Hakadah watched breathlessly as his uncle motioned the people to stop. There were outcries and shouts, but everyone obeyed his command and stood nervously while the flames rushed and roared down upon them.

Then Mysterious Medicine quickly made a fire and, with the help of several other men, passed a torch through the grass in a long line. The new fire burst to life and momentarily towered over the helpless people.

But the swift wind was favoring them; almost at once the fire they had started rose up as tall and deadly as the wild flames that threatened them. When the two great fires met, they burst hundreds of feet into the air in a final, immense explosion of flames.

# BETRAYAL

It was the second winter after the massacre and the people were still in flight when a powerful blizzard overtook them. The sky filled with wind. Torrents of snow swirled through the wide flatlands of Dakota Territory. The daylight was suffocated by the storm. And in the night many stars filled the sky like glittering specters. The world turned blue and silent.

Here and there families lay down in the new snow. They covered themselves with many buffalo robes and stayed huddled together for a day and a night as the deep drifts slowly covered their bodies.

Though the snow grew very heavy as the blizzard raged above them, it kept them warm, and gradually it packed down around their bodies so they were able to doze peacefully in the solitude of their white underworld.

Then the silence began to drone all around. And their world filled with soft, white light.

It was sunrise.

Hakadah opened his eyes uncertainly and gazed upward through the luminous snow that covered him. The storm had ended and now a brilliant light streamed down through the deep drifts, beckoning him to the surface as he carefully dug his way out.

The sunshine was dazzling. The endless white plains glowed and glittered. The world looked as if it had been just born. Hakadah crawled into the daylight and turned in a wide circle, peering in wonderment at the immensity of the frozen prairie.

The storm was over, and another trouble emerged.

Famine haunted the encampment. The old people denied themselves in order to make the food last as long as possible for the children. As they emerged from their cover of snow, they sniffed the air for a trace of game. They searched the ground for fresh tracks, but there were no animals except the frail little brown birds that flitted through the cloudless air.

The women went out into the deep snow, staggering to and fro in the hope of finding something for the children to eat. Meanwhile the men gathered around Mysterious Medicine and Many Lightnings and quietly discussed the fate of the little band of Indians.

"Someone must travel to the place called Winnipeg, where the soldiers of the United States will not follow." Mysterious Medicine said solemnly, looking anxiously into his brother's face. "There he must trade some of our best robes for food. Otherwise all of our people will perish."

"But it will take more than one person," Many Lightnings responded with a gesture toward the robes. "There must be many robes if we are to bring back enough provisions for our survival. So two or three men must go to Winnipeg."

"Yes, it is true," the elders agreed.

"Three men must go to Winnipeg."

Hakadah's father, Many Lightnings, volunteered to make the difficult journey. "And," he announced, "I will take my two oldest sons, Noma and Okha. They will lead the travois loaded with buffalo robes."

All the leaders agreed, and the preparations began at once for the departure. When Hakadah and Uncheedah returned to the camp from their hunt for food, the men announced the plan, and the grandmother wept at the thought of such a perilous adventure for her son.

"Hakadah is already motherless," she sobbed to Many Lightnings. "Surely you will not take his brothers from him too. Surely you, his father, will not go on such a dangerous trip! If something should happen to you who will be left to look after him?"

"I have volunteered to go and I must do it," Many Lightnings replied to his old mother, continuing to load the robes on the travois without looking at her.

"You are as stubborn as ever," Uncheedah exclaimed. "You will not listen to anyone once you have made up your mind! That is fine . . . but what about Hakadah, Chatanna, and me? What about your brother, Mysterious Medicine? Have you asked us how we will live if you are captured or killed? And what about the sons you are taking with you on this terrible adventure? Will you sacrifice them too?"

"Someone must go for food or none of us will live," Many Lightnings said resolutely. "I know this in my heart. And I must do what my heart tells me to do."

"Is there no room in your heart for us?" Uncheedah whispered.

"I must do whatever I know is right. And this journey is right."

The grandmother nodded her head and looked sadly at her willful son. She would not speak again.

The afternoon faded into evening while the men prepared to leave the camp. Uncheedah staggered through the deep snow, mumbling ferociously to herself as she continued to search for any morsel with which to feed Hakadah. As it was growing dark she disappeared into a thicket, and when she finally returned to the camp, she was smiling.

"Look!" she shouted to the women who came running out into the snow to meet her. "Birds! I have caught six birds!"

They were pathetic little brown creatures, half starved during the blizzard, but the mothers wept with joy as they hurried to the cooking fire and prepared the first food the people had had in several days.

The six frail birds served as dinner for six families. The fathers and mothers pressed their lips together and grimly declined their share of food, watching thankfully as their little ones ate.

Hakadah grinned with delight as he devoured his portion of the meal—one skinny little wing of a charred brown bird. It was not much to eat, but he looked up into his grandmother's eyes and smiled widely, feeling grateful for her sacrifice and proud of her skill as a hunter.

That night Hakadah's father, Many Lightnings, and his two oldest sons rode away into the bleak flatlands, heading against the wind toward Canada, the land of the Cold Maker.

Hakadah stood beside Uncheedah and Chatanna and watched them as they vanished into the darkness. A terrible sensation swept over him, and he cried out fearfully, clutching his grandmother's side.

"Some day, Hakadah," the old woman murmured to the frightened child as she continued to gaze after her departing family, "you will be old enough to know my secrets and I will tell them to you." Then she sighed and shook her head in grief. "But if you should grow up to be stubborn and reckless and mean, then I will withhold these treasures of our people. For a holy man must be as open as the sky. His heart must be so wide that he can see into the past and into the future."

With this Uncheedah turned her eyes away from her firstborn son and looked down at Hakadah. She gazed at him as he stood in the snow beside her, so small and helpless and afraid. "You are a good boy and I pray, my child, that you grow up to be wise and daring—but not foolish and brave. Not stubborn and vain. It is good to be a warrior like your father, for he is very powerful. But, my child, do not forget that it is still better to be a holy person, for such holiness requires a daring of the mind!"

Then the winds came again, and a soft drone spread slowly over the cold world of blue snow and deep silence. The people huddled together miserably and waited for Many Lightnings and his sons to return with the provisions. But they did not come. The cold days passed in pain and sorrow, for there was nothing to eat and few robes remained to protect the people against the driving torrents of snow.

They lay numb and cold under the huge drifts, shivering and moaning until it was dawn. Then they fought their way to the surface of the frozen landscape and searched the great desolation for some sign of Many Lightnings and his sons. But still they did not come.

Many weeks later, when Mysterious Medicine and the men sat mumbling dolefully to one another, a lone rider appeared on the horizon. Everyone caught sight of that distant figure at the same time, but there was not a whisper in the camp as the people arose hesitantly and stood in the wind, watching the horseman slowly making his way through the deep snow.

Finally, when he was close enough for Uncheedah to see his face, she covered her head and wept. It was not Many Lightnings!

The rider was called Watching Horses, a surly half-breed who was always crazy with meanness and whiskey. In a drunken rage he had once killed a defenseless boy and had been cast out of the tribe.

Watching Horses was grinning as he rode into camp. Peering arrogantly down at Mysterious Medicine, who had ordered him into exile, he dismounted and, leering, held out his hand.

In it was the necklace of Many Lightnings.

Suddenly Uncheedah screamed and threw herself into the snow. The women wept as they tried to comfort her, but she would not cease her wild lamentation. She tore her hair and snatched a knife from one of the men, drawing it quickly across her arms and legs as she sobbed. The old people sent up their throbbing song of sorrow, and Uncheedah sat bleeding and weeping as she hacked off her long hair and shook it frantically at the sky.

Hakadah watched, pale and fearful, while his grandmother wailed.

"I know I am not wanted here," Watching Horses said as the men gathered to listen to the story he had brought back to his old enemies.

Many Lightnings and his two sons had been betrayed, he told them. In Mankato a half-breed had pointed them out as the leaders of the Minnesota Massacre. Before they could escape, the United States authorities had captured them. In the evening, when it was getting dark in the frozen wasteland of Minnesota, at the place where the white men drew the line between Canada and the United States, the soldiers had shot Many Lightnings and his sons. Watching Horses had seen the broken bodies of Noma and Okha, but all that remained of Many Lightnings was a broken necklace.

Mysterious Medicine turned away from Watching Horses and covered his face with his robe. In the camp the fires went out one by one as the old women wept. And when the moon came into the frozen sky, nothing could be heard across the endless prairie except the sound of their lament.

# Part Three

# In the Footsteps of the People

# HOMELAND

"As long as you or your brother Chatanna shall live," Mysterious Medicine told Hakadah, handing the child the necklace that belonged to Many Lightnings, "there is but one duty that you must fulfill. You must allow nothing to prevent you from avenging your father's murder. Chatanna is already determined to be a brave, and his uncle is training him in the ways of warriors. Now you must put all thoughts of becoming a holy man behind you. You must put your grandmother behind you. Nothing must occupy your thoughts but becoming a strong and daring warrior so that you may fight and kill the white man and avenge the death of Many Lightnings!"

Grandmother drew Hakadah toward her as she looked disapprovingly at her son, Mysterious Medicine. "Enough talk of death and vengeance," she said sternly. "All you teach this child is anger. It is enough that Chatanna has been made to hate everyone! If he lived here with us I would not allow his thoughts to be filled with rage and vengeance!"

With this remark Uncheedah embraced Hakadah and smiled warmly into his face. "There are things in the world besides vengeance. There is also the proud memory of your father. And there is also the gift of life that he gave to you, Hakadah. You forget, Mysterious Medicine," she whispered sadly to her son, "that Many Lightnings was my firstborn. You forget the tears I cried, the wounds I opened upon my arms and legs. The great lamentation I sang! But my grief shall not be turned into bitterness. And your grief shall not be used to poison this son of my firstborn child!"

"But it is the duty of a son—" Mysterious Medicine began sternly.

Uncheedah interrupted him with a single gesture and said: "It is also the duty of a son to obey his mother. Let us hear no more of this. It is a time for celebration, for we have returned at last to the woodlands, to the familiar forests and lakes of our ancestors. The snow is vanishing. The streams are full. The people have much food, and they have the comfort of the warm sun. Let us not bring old sorrows with us into this new spring."

It was the first thaw, and everywhere there was the perpetual music of melting ice pelting the snow from above, collecting into tiny trickles that widened into frosty streams and swollen brooks. The sound of the water was everywhere, dripping, splashing, and babbling among the rocks.

With the first thaw everyone's thoughts turned to the annual sugarmaking, an activity that delighted the women, old men, and children of the camp. But it was also time for the young men to attend to their seasonal responsibilities. Mysterious Medicine, respecting his mother's wishes, turned Hakadah's training over to her care while he and the other men went off on the spring fur hunt.

"I shall say no more," he told Uncheedah as he bid her goodbye, "but that does not change the duty of a son to avenge the murder of his father!"

"Ai!" the old woman said impatiently, ". . . you are more stubborn than your poor brother! Look out that you do not end as he did and break your mother's heart! Go now," she murmured, an expression of affection filling her eyes, "and may the animals be generous to you so you may bring back many fine furs."

When the men had left the spring encampment, Uncheedah and Hakadah hiked across the puddles to the old bark sugarhouse abandoned there by the Ojibwa. It stood in the midst of a fine grove of maples. The hut was still filled with snow as well as the withered leaves of many autumns. It had to be cleared and cleaned before it would be ready for the sugarmaking.

"Ai . . ." Uncheedah murmured, "in Minnesota we had such a beautiful sugarhouse! How I miss those good days!"

But soon the sadness left, and she began to sing and smile as she worked. Everyone was happy except Hakadah. He was lonely, for he missed his brother Chatanna. Ever since the escape from the soldiers he rarely got to play with him.

"Where is Chatanna?" the child asked. "And why can't he come and live with us, Uncheedah?"

His grandmother shook her head, but she did not respond.

"I have no one," Hakadah murmured.

"Ai, you have me and you have Mysterious Medicine. Are we not family enough for one boy?" the old woman sighed with a sad look in her face.

"But there is no one my own age—no brothers or sisters," Hakadah complained.

"Shame on you," Uncheedah said. "All the children of the band are your brothers and sisters! They love you and are your good companions. And you have your little cousin, Oesedah, who comes to stay with us; and Chatanna is a good brother to you."

"But he never comes to our lodge. He stays with our uncle and he gets to go hunting with the men. And I have no one," Hakadah insisted.

"Chatanna is older than you are, and his uncle thinks of nothing but making him into a powerful warrior. All my sons can think of nothing but their proud ancestors, and all of them live for nothing but glory. If only they understood that their father, Chief Cloud Man, was both a brave man and a man of great kindness and love, they would not be so anxious for war!" Uncheedah exclaimed.

"But why doesn't Chatanna come and live with us? Why can't we be friends?"

"You are too young, Hakadah. Maybe when you are older and have won honor—then your brother will come to you and want to be your companion. But now you must be contented with who and what you are. You must welcome the person you are becoming instead of wanting to be someone else. Only in that way can you win a place in the world."

"But Chatanna . . ." Hakadah began.

"Chatanna is another person. Chatanna is not Hakadah. You must accept that, my child, or you will have nothing but sorrow in your life," she told him. "Your brother Chatanna has been very good to you. He taught you lacrosse and he taught you to run as fast as the antelope. Have you forgotten? Have you forgotten all he has given to you? He is older and must have his own friends and his own life. Now do you understand?" Grandmother asked patiently.

For a long time Hakadah was silent, and then he glanced discontentedly at his grandmother and nodded that he understood.

"Ai," Uncheedah said with a smile, trying to cheer the bewildered child. "Now we will make the sugar of the maple tree!"

The most important utensils for making sugar were the big iron and brass kettles in which the maple sap was boiled. But many of these kettles had been left behind during the long flight from the soldiers, and so the people had to buy from traders or beg and borrow from relatives. Everything else needed for the sugarmaking could be made.

Uncheedah was a generous woman with whom the elders gladly shared their belongings, and soon the kettles had been assembled in the sugarhouse. When this was done all the old women worked together to fell a maple tree in which they hollowed out a space to hold the sap that would be gathered.

While Uncheedah and her friends hacked at the pulpy heart of the maple log, Hakadah sat happily in the snow and created the little troughs of basswood and basins of birchbark that his grandmother had taught him to make. These troughs and basins would receive the sweet drops of sap that trickled from the trees as they awakened into spring.

The snow was still deep, and had a very hard crust upon which the people could walk quickly as they gathered a good supply of fuel for the sugar fires. They would not have much time to collect wood once the sap began to flow. Soon the mornings turned warm. The sunshine bounded off the ice as it began to melt. Then the showers commenced, carrying off most of the snow and bloating the river with churning white water.

Now the women began to test the trees, moving among them with an axe in hand, striking a single quick blow just hard enough to break the bark and see if the sap would flow from the wound.

As each maple began to trickle its rich, sweet resin, Hakadah set the basins under each tree and his grandmother drove a hardwood chip deep into the cut that the axe had made. From the corners of this chip, first slowly and then in a constant trickle, the sap flowed into the collecting basins.

Uncheedah laughed merrily and thrust her hands onto her hips, as she gazed contentedly at the numerous trees tapped for their precious sap.

The old woman was fully seventy, yet she was strong and handsome. The other elders were stout and slow, but Uncheedah was slender and agile. She was a leader among the women, for she understood the forest, and it had long been her special power to know just where to look for each edible plant. In her knowledge of the forest Uncheedah was wiser than most of the men. She understood the herbs that heal and the roots that give strength to children. Everyone respected Grandmother's wisdom of the forest, and they often came to her for aid and healing.

When her old husband, Chief Cloud Man, had died, she was still a young woman. She was descended from a haughty chieftain, and although women of her age and tribal position were expected to remarry, she preferred, despite several persistent suitors, to remain in solitude with the memory of her husband.

Hakadah was very proud of his grandmother, and he smiled brightly as he looked at her, standing there with her hands on her hips—so strong and handsome—surveying the preparations for sugarmaking.

"Now we must make the fire," Uncheedah exclaimed joyfully.

A long fire was made in the damp birchbark sugarhouse, and as the heat rose the wet wooden structure steamed and fumed, filling the air with its musky perfume. Hakadah inhaled deliriously, for it was the pungent smell of spring and it foretold the return of the leaves and the sweet grass and the butterflies.

Now the kettles were carefully suspended over the blazing fire, and the sap everyone had collected and stored in the log canoe was ladled into the big pots and allowed to simmer very slowly.

This sugary aroma mixed in the pungent smoky air while the boys and girls grinned widely in anticipation of the sweets that would soon be ready. Each boy was put in charge of one kettle. It was his duty to see that the fire burned brightly but not too brightly, for too much flame would cause the sap to boil over. And finally, when the simmering brown liquid became a thick syrup, it was his duty to test it by dropping a bit of it with a wooden paddle onto the snow. If the sap turned quickly into a hard pellet, then the syrup was ready.

Hakadah let out a shout of pleasure when the kettle in his charge yielded a large, firm lump of sugar, and Uncheedah hurried to his side and began at once to make cakes of many different shapes in little molds of birchbark. Some of the sugar she pulverized and packed away in rawhide boxes. The smaller candies were saved for special feasts, when sugar was eaten with wild rice or parched corn and pounded dried meat.

When the work was done Uncheedah gave Hakadah a large piece of the delicious candy. Then she embraced him and said: "The trees have been kind to us. The weather is good to us. We have had a spring that we shall remember!"

It was Hakadah's eighth summer. There were many good days for the people. The spring fur hunters had been blessed with the generosity of the animals, and the maples had given an abundance of syrup from which the women had made much maple sugar. The patches of potatoes and maize were fertile, and the birds, fat on berries and bugs, made the camp joyful with their many songs.

Now it was the time of the midsummer celebration of the old, free days of the tribe.

The invitations to the festivities were in the form of bundles of tobacco, and were sent out by the host, Blue Earth, chief of the band. Over the days many acceptances were sent back to Blue Earth by the various bands. There would be many people at the festival, and as the time approached Hakadah and his grandmother were very excited.

"You are a big fellow now," Uncheedah murmured into his ear as she gave him his dinner, "and you must make your uncle Mysterious Medicine as proud of you for your valor as I am already proud of you for your wisdom. There will be many different games in which you may win favor and honor. If you prepare yourself for the games with fasting and exercise I know you will bring great joy to your uncle."

"I will do it!" Hakadah exclaimed. "The most important game of all is the lacrosse contest. For that game they will select the best runners. And, Grandmother, I am the fastest runner of all the boys. So I will win for Mysterious Medicine! I will make Mysterious Medicine and Chatanna very proud of me!"

In a few days the village was bustling with the newly arrived guests. The meat of wild game that had been dried and put away during the previous fall in anticipation of this joyous feast time, was taken out. There was wild rice and the choicest of dried venison, as well as freshly dug turnips, ripe purple berries, and an abundance of fresh meat.

Along the edge of the woods the lodges were pitched in groups and semicircles, each band distinct from the others. The tipi of the festival's host, Blue Earth, was located in a place of honor. Just over the entrance of his dwelling was a painted red and yellow image of a pipe and the rising Sun.

"These pictures," Uncheedah told her grandson, "are a welcome to all people who live under the bright Sun!"

Then the old woman hurried Hakadah back to their own duties, for within the lodge of Blue Earth a meeting was being held that no one dared to disturb.

"Hush, my child," Uncheedah whispered. "We must not bother the holy people, for they are within the tipi appointing the medicine man who will make the balls to be used in the lacrosse contest."

No sooner had Hakadah and his grandmother returned to their lodge than the camp crier ceremonially announced that the great honor of making the lacrosse balls had been conferred upon old Chankpee-yuhah—Keeps the Club.

Chankpee-yuhah was proud of his appointment and spent the

afternoon smiling broadly as he received the good wishes of the people. Then toward evening he came forward into the camp circle, calling out to all the young men. They willingly crowded around Keeps the Club, anxious to hear what he had to say, for he was a man of powerful and imposing physique who had won the confidence and admiration of the young men by his majestic manner and his fine personal appearance.

When the young people had assembled, Keeps the Club made a wide gesture, pointing at one young man after another until at last his hand stopped abruptly. "Come forward," Keeps the Club said in his most ceremonious voice.

Hakadah shook his head in delight, for the old holy man was pointing at him.

Hakadah paused for a moment, glancing at the other young men; then he stepped into the circle with his black eyes wide in amazement.

While Keeps the Club drew himself up into an exalted posture and began to speak, he slowly plaited Hakadah's glossy black hair and wound it around his head into an elaborate headdress. He placed a bit of swan's down in each of Hakadah's ears, and then he painted the boy's face and chest.

"People of the Leaf Band, this boy is your child. He boasts that he can run as fast as the antelope, that he can outrun the Ojibwa as a rabbit can outrun the snail. Hakadah, I therefore dedicate to you this red ball."

The young men murmured and glanced at Hakadah with looks of admiration and envy. Meanwhile Keeps the Club called another boy into the circle, and he too was painted and ornamented while Keeps the Club spoke again: "Son of the Canoe Band," he said solemnly, "you are a strong young man and you claim that no one has a lighter foot than you. To you I dedicate this black ball." Then Keeps the Club looked at the two young men. "The pride of your people is in you. One of you will win while the other will lower his eyes and bow his head when the game is over. Those are the ways of fortune."

The ground selected for the final and most important contest between the Leaf and the Canoe bands was on a narrow strip of land between a lake and the wide river. It was a large meadow without trees, ideal for the contest, and it afforded the spectators a fine vantage. The people had already gathered along the choicest knolls and were waiting anxiously for the game to begin. Meanwhile, the warriors appointed to keep the crowd orderly strutted proudly back and forth down the length of the meadow. Their bodies as well as their shields and war clubs were handsomely painted with brilliantly colored sacred images. They were a handsome troop of policemen and were also very strict enforcers of the rules of the contest, not allowing anyone, no matter what his or her rank, to venture within the limits of the field.

With the hooting of the heralds and the excited murmurs of the people, the players assembled. Those who were massive and powerful were stationed at the halfway ground, while the fast, slender runners were assigned to the backfields. It was a fantastic sight. And Hakadah was overcome with excitement. He looked out among the many agile bodies, stripped to breechclout and painted in blazing imitations of the rainbow. Some of the young men had imprinted the glittering Milky Way across their tawny torsos, while others had painted their chests with white lightning. Hakadah spent much time and effort making the image of a swift red bird upon his body. He was exceedingly proud of that crimson creature as he confidently took his place among the runners of his band.

He stood in the midst of the magnificent young men, unable to think of anything but his deep desire to bring honor to his people. He wanted to be swift and strong, to be daring and cunning. He wanted to make his uncle Mysterious Medicine proud of him. And he prayed to be as sleek and agile as the four-legged creatures that Uncheedah loved.

But as Hakadah waited for the contest to begin, his legs trembled and he felt sick. Just as his fear mounted into a terrible panic, he felt someone touch him on the shoulder. It was his brother Chatanna. He did not speak. He simply smiled confidently at Hakadah. And suddenly the child was strong and eager for the contest.

In the middle of the field were four men of magnificent form. They posed expectantly as a fifth man approached them. He paused for just a moment, then threw his head back, gazing up into the farthest heavens, and called out in a clear, melodious voice.

Instantly the little black ball went up between the players while the crowd let out great war whoops.

The leader of each team leaped high into the air and desperately tried to catch the ball in the air. At once the guards rushed forward, and for a time hundreds of lacrosse sticks recklessly swung and swerved and bashed at one another.

Hakadah stood his ground, anxiously awaiting his moment. All he could see was a mass of wriggling bodies and a heap of fantastic painted emblems twisting together in a cloud of dust.

Suddenly the ball rose up like a bird and shot swiftly through the air toward the goal of the Canoe team. Their fans erupted with cheers that echoed from the cliffs, and Hakadah's heart sank for fear that his team might lose. But a Leaf guard made a fantastic leap and prevented the ball from entering the bag at the goal.

Fifteen or twenty players slammed into each other with a terrific thud, and the ball struck the ground and rolled away in the confusion. But a daring Leaf player pounced upon it like a cat and slipped out of the grasp of his frantic opponents.

A mighty cheer thundered through the meadow.

The warrior who had intercepted the ball started down the field, dodging a flood tide of burly Canoe players as he attempted to gain ground. He was transformed by his determination, springing and leaping over the endless succession of opponents who tried to seize him or block his way or throw him to the ground. But he evaded them all.

Now every opposing player was upon his heels, while those of his own team did everything they could to clear the way for the madly running warrior.

He crashed to the ground and was buried under the onslaught of massive bodies. He had gained only fifty paces despite his heroic efforts.

Thus the game went. First one team and then the other would gain an advantage, and all the while the young men sweated and strained with tremendous courage and strength. Eventually the herald proclaimed that it was time to change the ball, for no victory was in sight for either side.

After a few moments' rest, the game was resumed. This time the red ball was tossed into the air, and as it plummeted back to earth one of the rushers caught it and began his long race for the goal. The meadow was now the scene of the wildest confusion and excitement yet. The Leaf rusher was flying across the grass, bounding over blockers, twisting around opponents, wrestling out of their grip, and racing headlong toward the north goal.

For just a moment the flight of the ball was checked, and a desperate struggle ensued while cheers and bellows went up from the crowd. The red ball rose and fell and rose again. It had not come down once during all the mayhem, for there were more than a hundred young men scrambling for it.

Suddenly a slender figure shot out of the knot of bodies.

"Look out!" a player shouted. "Look out! He's got the ball!"

But it was too late. The little sphere was firmly nestled in

Hakadah's hand. He threw down his lacrosse stick and was dashing like an antelope for the goal.

He flew across the soft earth, feeling the wind in his face. He threw his body into space, as his heart boomed and his legs ached with power. Now he had cleared almost all the guards. There were only two more—lurching, weaving to and fro in front of him. They were the fleetest runners of the Canoe Band! And Hakadah instantly realized the danger.

As he approached them his blood pounded in his throat and his head was full of the bellows from the crowd. He opened his mouth wide and gasped for air as he plummeted toward the two oncoming guards. In another moment there would be victory or defeat. The faces of the two guards loomed closer, filled with blind determination as they prepared to spring at Hakadah. For a moment his impulse was to slacken his pace or swerve around his ferocious oncoming opponents, but instead he pressed forward directly into their path at full speed.

There was a crash! Then an immense cheer! The two Canoe players had collided, and the swift Hakadah had barreled through them, making the goal! He had won the contest for his exuberant people!

The commotion at the victors' camp was enormous. The young men surrounded Hakadah and showered him with admiration and affection. The old men embraced him and the women sent up shrill victory whoops. Then there was the sound of the drum, and the people became silent as the criers hurried through the camp announcing an honor ceremony that was to be conducted by the elders.

After a vast circle was formed by all the people, the members of the common council assembled and sat majestically in the center, looking around at the elated crowd. When silence fell over the massive audience, Blue Earth slowly arose, and in a few eloquent words assured his guests that it was not conceit or selfishness that enabled his braves to carry off the honors of the contest. The game of lacrosse, he reminded them, was a friendly contest in which each band must give its best efforts. The winning or the losing was not important, Blue Earth exclaimed. "It is the skill of the game and the determination of its players that makes this contest holy and memorable among the tribes."

There was a loud *Ho-o-o-o* that swelled from the throats of winners and losers, reverberating up from the forest and down the wide expanse of the river.

"In memory of this day," Blue Earth continued, "a boy will be given his name."

Shuddering from exhaustion and pale with anxiety, Hakadah was now brought into the great circle. Cheer after cheer went up for the awestruck child as he gazed around at the hundreds of people who smiled upon him. His heart beat quickly with immense joy as his eyes fixed upon Chatanna and Mysterious Medicine. Their faces were glowing with admiration.

"*Ye-sa*—'Winner'—that shall be the name of this young man," the holy man Blue Earth intoned in the reverent silence of the assembly. "Be brave, my son; be patient, and you shall always be victorious! Your name is henceforth *Yesa*!"

# LESSONS

He fell in love with the wings of birds, the bright light of spring dancing upon them in the morning. Without looking up he knew that the sparrows were bathing in the hot Sun. Just from the happy voices of the children, he knew that the willows grew greener. And with every gust of wind the butterflies changed places in the branches, beating their translucent wings into colors.

These were the most wonderful days. But they were also days of much learning, for Yesa was no longer a boy. Now that he had earned a name for himself, he left behind the games of children—the mock battles against the bees, the wrestling, and the make-believe hunting parties. Now all the battles were real, and the search for food was a serious business that demanded skill and wisdom.

"You have much to learn, Yesa, before you will be truly a man," Mysterious Medicine told him. "And you must listen carefully to all that I tell you."

His uncle was his teacher until his fifteenth winter. He was strict and solemn, but Yesa admired his knowledge and gave great attention to the lessons given to him by Mysterious Medicine.

"Yesa," his uncle would say, "look closely at everything you see. Do not let anything miss your attention."

And in the evening, when Yesa returned to the lodge, his uncle questioned his observations.

"On which side of the trees is the lighter bark? On which side do the branches grow most regularly?"

Then Mysterious Medicine would ask Yesa to describe all the new birds that he had seen during the day. The young man would speak of their color or the shape of their bill or their song. And then his uncle would give each its proper name, and Yesa repeated it until he had committed it to memory.

"Yesa," Mysterious Medicine would ask, "how do you know if there are fish in a lake?"

Anxious to please his uncle, Yesa blurted out the first thing that came into his head. "Because they jump out of the water for flies!"

Mysterious Medicine smiled patiently and then he said, "What do you think of the little pebbles grouped together under the shallow water? And what has made the pretty curved marks in the sandy bottom, and the little sandbanks? Where do you often see the birds that eat fish?"

"Ah," murmured the young man apologetically, ". . . now I understand. These are all the signs that tell us that fish live in a lake."

The old man nodded slowly. "You must follow the example of the *Shunktokecha*—the wolf, my child. Even when he is chased and must run for his very life, he will always pause for just a moment to take one more look at you before he dashes away. So you too, Yesa, must learn to take a second look at everything you see. You can learn much from the animals. But you should watch them silently and unobserved. I have been a witness to their courtships and their quarrels and have learned many of their secrets in this way. I once saw a terrifying battle between a pair of grizzly bears and three buffalos—a very foolish fight for the bears, for it was then the Moon of strawberries, when the buffalo sharpen and polish their big horns for the bloody contests they wage among themselves. From these observations of the four-legged ones you learn to be a hunter and a warrior, for the animals know more than we will ever know and it is the wise person who learns as much from them as he can. Do you understand?" Mysterious Medicine asked in a whisper.

Yesa nodded as he watched every gesture and grimace of his uncle.

"In hunting," the old man continued solemnly, "you will be guided by the habits of the animal you seek. Always remember that a moose stays in swampy, low land or between high mountains near a spring or a lake. When you are confronted by a bear or a wildcat who shows signs of attacking you, you must make him understand that you have seen him and are aware of what he intends to do. If you rush such an animal with a sharp spear he will turn and run, for no beast will face such an attack unless he is cornered and wounded. There is, however, one exception: the gray wolf will attack fiercely when he is very hungry. But their courage depends entirely upon their numbers. In this they are much like white men. One or two wolves will never attack a man. But a pack of wolves is deadly, because each cowardly wolf takes his courage from the group. This is a failure of the wolves, for a creature must take courage from himself."

These were the teachings of Mysterious Medicine, a man widely known as one of the greatest hunters of the tribe. And it was from this uncle that Yesa learned much of warring and hunting and the quest of manhood.

All boys were expected to endure hardship as part of their education. A young man had to be strong and fit; he had to be able to go without food and water without displaying weakness; he had to be capable of long-distance running, and he was required regularly to traverse a pathless and alien countryside without losing his way by either day or night. All these abilities were required of any young man who hoped to be a warrior.

Sometimes Mysterious Medicine would abruptly awaken Yesa, in the early morning before the sun had arisen, and challenge his nephew to fast with him all day. Yesa had no choice; he was expected to accept such contests as part of the ordeal of becoming an adult. He and his uncle would blacken their faces with charcoal so everyone in the village would know they were fasting, and then they would go out among the people, who tempted them with delicacies. Poor Yesa was especially taunted with food and water until he was ready to lose his temper or give in to temptation. But mercifully the sun would finally reach the western hills, and the difficult fast would be over.

Often, no sooner had the exhausted Yesa fallen to sleep than he would be suddenly awakened by loud war whoops.

"Wha . . . wha . . . what's happening!" he would yelp as he leaped to his feet.

It was Mysterious Medicine who had snuck up on Yesa and shouted the war cries. He expected his nephew to awaken with perfect presence of mind, always ready to grasp a weapon and to give a shrill whoop in reply. If Yesa failed to respond properly, if he were startled or sleepy or confused, then Mysterious Medicine would ridicule him and say that he would never become a warrior.

No sooner had Yesa accustomed himself to being roused from a sound sleep by war cries than his crafty uncle changed his tactics and would shoot off his gun just outside the lodge. But eventually Yesa managed to respond with alertness to every trick his uncle could devise. And finally Mysterious Medicine smiled proudly at his nephew. Yesa smiled back, knowing his uncle's pleasure meant he was becoming stronger and wiser each day, and that soon he would be old enough and skillful enough to join a war party.

* * *

Whenever the Indians of the Plains went on the warpath, it was their custom to test the young warriors, putting them through many ordeals before they ever came face to face with the enemies. And so it happened that Yesa and his brother, Chatanna, were put to the test by their elders. When they were near a hostile Indian camp, the brothers were selected to go after the water, though the creek was dangerously close to the enemies.

Yesa was ready for the challenge. Together with Chatanna, he picked his way through the dark woods, dipped the pail into the water as quickly and as quietly as possible, and then hurried back to camp. The two brothers' hearts leaped at every crackling twig, every hoot of the owls, until at last they reached the tipi of their uncle.

Mysterious Medicine smiled proudly at both of them, and they breathed a sigh of relief as they turned to join the men around the fire. But their uncle was not finished with their test. Slowly he turned the bucket on its side and spilled the contents on the ground.

"Yes, Yesa and Chatanna, it is true. I think you are going to be very brave men," he said as he emptied out the precious contents of the pail. "And so now you will fill the bucket a second time and show twice as much courage."

By the time the brothers returned to the encampment of their people the second time, they were so exhausted they could not eat. Chatanna slouched off to the lodge of his uncle, while Yesa returned to the tipi of his grandmother.

"Ai!" she exclaimed as she embraced him. "But do not forget. To be a warrior is good," she murmured as she led Yesa to his bed, "but to be wise and generous is also good!"

And then, as she put wood on the fire and squatted over the kettle, rocking to and fro on her heels, she gazed lovingly at her grandson. "Close your eyes, my strong-hearted child," she whispered, "and I will tell you a marvelous story. This is the tale of the *Hetunkala*—the field mice who live in the sky. Each night the mice saw the little sliver of the Moon grow larger. Yes, each night they saw the Moon hanging in the enormous black sky, growing so heavy that she began to fall. It was then, many years ago, that the mice nibbled gently upon her sides until she was small enough to rise once again . . . high into the deepest heavens! But one terrible night," Uncheedah murmured, "the *Hetunkala* nibbled too eagerly, leaving scars upon the silver Moon. And so they were hurled down to the Earth, and they lost their special place in the sky. And ever since that day, they have gathered when the Moon is full, trying to find their way back among the Stars."

The grandmother smiled and touched Yesa's black hair. "Be strong of heart . . . be patient!" she whispered as he drifted to sleep. "But above all, Yesa, learn to dream, for there is no secret and no power in a man who does not know how to dream."

The wings of birds fluttered in the moonlight. The willows grew greener. And with every gust of wind the butterflies changed places in the branches of his mind, beating their translucent wings into colors and dreams as he slept.

And then it was morning.

Chatanna was the brother with whom Yesa now passed all his days. Though they had lived with different grandmothers ever since the death of their mother, they were now constant companions as they approached manhood. Their two older brothers had perished with their father. Of the four sons, they were the last, and they naturally shared many problems and secrets. They played together, slept together, and ate together. They also shared many dreams. And as Chatanna was three summers older, Yesa looked up to him and often sought his advice on the many mysteries of the world.

Yesa also had a cousin who was four summers younger than

he, and though he had known her all his life, it was not until these years of his initiation into manhood that he began to take notice of her.

She was called Oesedah.

Although Oesedah had a mother who looked after her with great affection and care, it was Uncheedah who had become her chaperone and teacher. And so during the same days that Mysterious Medicine attended to the education of Yesa, Uncheedah taught little Oesedah all the knowledge that young women were expected to know before they could become wives. From a small and awkward little girl, Oesedah was being transformed daily into a very handsome woman.

When Yesa was not out in the woods with Chatanna, he would sit at home with Oesedah. His beautiful cousin always had a hundred urgent questions ready for him. Some of these inquiries were simple for Yesa to answer because they dealt with everyday tribal matters, but some of his cousin's questions were very mysterious and to answer them took considerable wisdom.

Uncheedah had skillfully dodged these difficult questions by telling Oesedah: "Yesa ought to know that—he is a man and I am not! You should ask him."

The truth of the matter, however, was that Uncheedah had herself already explained the answers to many of these "manly" questions to Yesa. It was Grandmother's way of encouraging the young people to talk to each other and to try to understand and solve their problems by themselves. Often Uncheedah quizzed Yesa, Chatanna, and Oesedah together, urging them to answer her questions together, and in this way learn how much power there could be in acting as a group rather than as individuals.

"What bird shows most judgment in caring for its young?" Uncheedah asked.

At once Chatanna exclaimed: "The eagle!"

Yesa, on the other hand, was silent for a long time. He was

confused—so many birds came into his mind all at once. He couldn't decide upon an answer. Finally he declared: "It is the oriole!"

"Ai . . ." Uncheedah said with a grin. "Now tell me, Chatanna, what proof do you have that the eagle is the best parent?"

Chatanna spoke with complete confidence. "The eagle is the wisest of all birds. Its nest is made in the safest possible place, upon a high and inaccessible cliff. It provides its young with much fresh meat. And in its mountaintop nest it has the freshest of air. The eagle is brought up under the spell of the grandest scenes and inspired with lofty feelings and great bravery. It sees that all other beings live beneath it and that eagles are the children of the king of the birds. A young eagle shows the spirit of a warrior while still in its nest. Being exposed to the weather the young eagle becomes hardy and strong. It is accustomed to the voice of the Thunderbird and the sighing of the Great Mystery. The eagle cannot help being noble because its parents select the most lofty place in which it is born. Isn't that so, Uncheedah?" Chatanna concluded with great excitement in his voice.

"Ai," she murmured as she smiled at Chatanna and then slowly looked at Yesa and awaited his speech in behalf of the orioles.

At first Yesa was staggered by the nobility of Chatanna's fine speech, and he could not bring himself to speak. But soon he recovered his confidence with the help of Oesedah, who said: "Wait until Yesa tells us about the loveliness of the oriole's home!"

"My grandmother, it was you who said that a mother who has a gentle voice will have children of a good disposition. I think the oriole is that kind of parent. It provides both sunshine and shadow for its young. Its nest is suspended from a bough where it is rocked by every gentle wind; and this nest is lined with soft things both deep and warm so that the featherless little birds do not suffer the cold."

"That is just like white people," Chatanna interrupted with annoyance. "That's just like them! And who cares about them! The eagle teaches its young to survive hardships. That is the Indian way!"

"Ai! Chatanna," Yesa exclaimed, "you have interrupted me before I have finished. Grandmother, surely I have the right to say what I wish to say."

"Ai," Uncheedah agreed, "you have that right and your brother should be ashamed for a discourtesy we would not even offer an enemy, for each person must be heard. *That,* Chatanna, is the true Indian way!"

Chatanna lowered his head with embarrassment as Yesa continued to speak. "You would not have lived, Chatanna, if you had been exposed to the snow and the wind when you were a baby!" he said reproachfully to his brother. "The oriole shows wisdom in providing its children with a warm home. It also offers them love when they are young and need much love. Of all the birds the oriole has been the wisest, for it has created a nest unlike any other nest. It is love of their children that has inspired the oriole to invent such a marvelous nest, while it is only pride that makes the eagle raise its children in the freezing heights of the mountains!"

The brothers peered anxiously at Uncheedah for her decision.

"You are good boys and you have learned to think and to speak your minds, and that is more important than being right."

"But which of us speaks the truth?" Chatanna insisted.

Grandmother laughed and touched both of her grandsons with a loving gesture. Then she said: "When we are wise and when we ponder many questions, it is not truth that we are seeking, my children. What we are seeking is meaning. And meaning and truth are not the same things."

To this remark Oesedah smiled brightly, for she seemed to grasp things that the brothers had great difficulty understanding. She was an odd little creature, with a heart so generous and good that she seemed at times more like one of the four-legged creatures than a young woman.

When autumn arrived Oesedah began living with Uncheedah and Yesa, for it was a difficult season and her family was so large there was not enough meat to go around. Mysterious Medicine was a great hunter and there was always enough food for everyone. And so Oesedah would come to the lodge of Uncheedah and stay through the fall months. The girl was lonely, however, as she was the only young female in the family. She often played by herself while Yesa and Chatanna were hunting with their uncle. There was one willow in particular that Oesedah visited regularly, holding long conversations with it, a portion of which she would afterward repeat to Yesa.

"That's ridiculous!" Chatanna would mutter. "Talking to a willow tree!"

But Yesa believed in such things, for he had often spoken to the animals. "What did the willow say?" he asked his cousin.

She blushed and explained that the willow was her husband. Some curious magic spell had compelled the young warrior she loved to assume the shape of a tree.

"But you must not tell Chatanna," she insisted, "because he cannot understand such things."

So Yesa never spoke of Oesedah's secret to Chatanna.

But for all of his bad temper and stubbornness Chatanna was a good and loyal friend, and Yesa loved him dearly. They shared many secrets and they depended upon each other's allegiance. They had pledged eternal friendship in Yesa's thirteenth summer. And they had sworn that they would go on their first warpath together and either win, or die, side by side.

Then one spring morning Mysterious Medicine took Chatanna
with him to the Canadian trading post on the Assiniboine River,
where the people often went to trade off furs for ammunition and
supplies.

When Mysterious Medicine returned to camp, Chatanna was
not with him!

Yesa was terrified that his brother had been killed, but his
uncle quickly explained what had taken place. A white Canadian
at the post with whom Mysterious Medicine did some trading
had six daughters but no sons. When he saw how handsome and
intelligent Chatanna was, he at once offered to adopt him.

"What?" Yesa exclaimed in sorrow. "Do you mean that you
have given my brother away?"

Uncheedah gave Yesa a stern look. He was not allowed to
speak to his uncle discourteously no matter how unhappy he
might be.

"The trader promised that we can go to see him whenever we
wish," Mysterious Medicine said. "And, as you know, by giving
this trader Chatanna we have greatly strengthened our friendship, for now our families are one."

Yesa turned away and could not speak.

He silently left the lodge and stood in the darkness, looking
into the north with a terrible pain in his heart.

For many long weeks he could not be consoled. Uncheedah
did everything to gladden her grandson, but a black shadow
hung over his face. His only companion was little Oesedah, with
whom he whispered beneath the willow on the river's narrow
bank.

"How could Chatanna desert me like that?" Yesa muttered.

"He did not want to do it," Oesedah insisted. "I know how
much he loved you! He would have come back to us if it were
possible. But he could not return. He has been changed into a
white man just as my husband was turned into a willow!"

Yesa did not speak. He sat sadly with his cousin under the wide branches of the tree until Uncheedah could no longer bear his silence.

"What is there to be done?" she murmured. "I too mourn the loss of that precious boy, but what can be done? Your uncle is a strong man with an unyielding will of his own, and neither you nor I can argue with him."

"But what will become of Chatanna?" Yesa cried out in pain.

For a moment the old woman's eyes filled with tears and she shook her head helplessly. "All the sons are lost but you, my pitiful last. And there is nothing Uncheedah can do about it. I would rather that he had been taken away by the Ojibwa. I would rather that he had been stolen by an enemy than by that trader, for now he will be taught the ways of the white man!" And again Uncheedah bowed her head and wept.

As the dark days passed Grandmother became so despondent that she would not speak or eat. The gloom of the lodge became unbearable, and at last Mysterious Medicine, shamed by the disapproving glances of his family, relented.

"Ai!" he groaned peevishly. "I will take him back! I will take him back! The next time I visit the trading post I will bring Chatanna home again, if only the three of you will bring this dismal behavior to an end!"

Yesa was delighted and warmly embraced his befuddled uncle.

"None of that . . . none of that!" Mysterious Medicine exclaimed. "You are too old to be fondling your uncle! So behave yourself and understand that you should be punished for having questioned my decision!"

"He is still a boy. . . ." Uncheedah softly protested, touching her angry son on the shoulder.

"No," Mysterious Medicine countered sternly, "he is a man, and if he wishes to be a warrior he must learn to obey his elders!

That is the first thing that a brave must learn. To weep and mourn your losses is beneath a true warrior. Yesa, you must learn to accept the commands of your elders! Never again will I permit you to contest my word!"

With these angry words, Mysterious Medicine left the lodge. Yesa's heart was crushed, for his uncle had never spoken to him so harshly, and despite his joy over the promised return of Chatanna, he was still deeply mortified.

But the reunion was not to be. The white trader was a cunning man. No sooner had he taken Chatanna into his family than he moved to a remote region of Canada.

Yesa never saw Chatanna again.

# FIRST OFFERING

Many summer days came and went. The leaves drifted from the aspen, gliding golden and dry in the autumn mornings. The cold winds descended upon the meadows and covered the sweet grass and the wild turnips. And through each of these many days, Yesa grieved the loss of his brother. Now there was no one with whom Yesa could practice lacrosse. There was no one with whom he could stalk rabbits in the woods. Oesedah had returned to the campfire of her own mother at the beginning of summer. Now when Uncheedah sat by the fire and repeated the tales of the people and questioned Yesa about the many mysteries of the world, there was no one with whom to match wits.

"Ai," Yesa moaned when his grandmother asked him what was troubling him. But he could not explain the sadness in his heart. He had no words for such pain.

Uncheedah gazed at him sympathetically. "There are many lessons to be learned in life," she whispered. "Many of these things may be learned in the good days, without hurt or harm. But the greatest wisdom can only be gained with great sorrow. We do not know why it should be so, but that is the way it is with us. From pain we learn courage. From sadness we learn generosity. From shame we learn dignity. From the longest winters come the greenest springs."

With these words of advice Uncheedah allowed herself a bu of emotion, warmly embracing the young man and smiling him. Then she went outside momentarily, and when she re turned to the lodge she was carrying a bundle.

"What is that?" Yesa inquired.

A small sound came from the bundle. Then a resounding yelp.

"Oh!" Yesa exclaimed with joy. It was a little yellow puppy, tightly wrapped in a bundle of soft skins.

"This little one is also lonely," Uncheedah said. "He is called Wabeda and he shall be a good friend."

The young man and the dog did indeed become the best of friends, and soon Yesa and Wabeda were bounding through the forest and splashing in the creeks, as happy and carefree as Yesa had been in the happy days before Chatanna had gone away.

Again the summer days came and went. The golden aspens shook their leaves into the swift fall wind. Winter bounded across the mountains, bringing storms and many cold days.

In the year of the "coldest winter," the band camped on the Mouse River, a wide stream that wound its way through a narrow valley just west of Turtle Mountain. The elders claimed that there had never been a colder winter in the history of the people.

There was a great snowfall, and the cold was so bitter that no one ventured from the lodges unless it was essential. The snow was far too deep for hunting, and the main body of buffalo had moved out of the valley, across the Missouri, where the hunters could not venture without grave difficulties.

Fortunately the prior summer had provided excellent hunting, so the women had prepared and dried an abundance of buffalo meat. And despite the wickedly cold weather there were many black-tailed deer and tall elk along the river, and grizzly bears could easily be found in the open country. But though there was ample food, still it proved to be a hard winter.

The ponies could not be used in the drifts. They simply could not make their way in the deep snow. The men were forced to hunt on large snowshoes. Then a sudden thaw formed a thin crust on the snow that would scarcely hold the weight of a man. It was during this "coldest winter" that the people resorted to hunting with dogsleds.

Yesa had been skating on the lake, gliding across the ice on skates that were nothing more than strips of basswood bark bound tightly to his feet. Wabeda, though already grown and wise, was nonetheless amazed by his master's ability to float over the frozen ground while he himself slipped and slid on all four paws every time he ventured out onto the lake.

Yesa laughed at his dog's awkwardness until the wretched animal gave him a look of disapproval.

"Ai, Wabeda, do not be so proud. As Grandmother always tells us, we have to learn to live with every day."

Wabeda did not seem placated by his young master's wisdom, and commenced to prance and bark along the shore until Yesa glided to his side and consented to return to the camp.

It was intensely cold. The trees cracked all about them as they hurried toward their warm tipi. The ice-coated branches waved in the breeze and popped and resounded like rifle shots.

As soon as Yesa reached the lodge, he took off his frozen moccasins and put on dry ones. Then he hunched over the bright fire and smiled while Uncheedah sang to herself and prepared his dinner.

"Where have you been and what have you and Wabeda been doing all morning?" she asked as she placed before him some delicious roast venison in a big wooden bowl.

"I have been skating on the lake."

"Ai," she said as she watched her grandson hungrily empty the bowl, "you were gone so long you almost missed the hunt with dogsleds! Even now the men are preparing to go hunting on the thin crust of ice by using dogsleds instead of horses."

This news excited Yesa so much that he did not finish his meal. At once he called to Wabeda and they rushed out of the lodge. They quickly located the men and watched expectantly as they prepared to go off on a most unusual hunt.

The sleds were made of buffalo ribs and hickory saplings. The runners were bound with rawhide, which allowed them to slip smoothly over the icy crust that covered the entire valley. No sooner were these sleds ready for use than the hunting scouts reported that they had spotted a small, stranded group of buffalo. Everyone had his dog team ready, and with much barking and tugging and shouting the hunting party got underway.

Wabeda was too independent to be of any use as part of a dog team, so Yesa threw him into a sled and leaped in after him, hanging onto the sides as they lurched over the meadow and went sailing along over the ice.

The men had their bows and arrows, and a few had guns. The great buffalo lumbered about in the drifts and could not run fast enough to evade the hunters. The dogs with their drivers soon caught up with the burly beasts, and the men brought many of them down.

The hunters left the sleds and waded through the snow and ice on their large snowshoes, in order to finish off the fallen animals that had not yet died. One of these was the biggest of the buffalo, who stood in the snow severely wounded.

"I shall crawl up to him from behind and stab him," said Wamedee, one of the bravest of the hunters. "We cannot wait out here in the cold for him to die."

The others agreed, and as Wamedee took out his knife and held it between his teeth, Yesa watched intently.

The brave hunter very slowly approached the buffalo from behind, crawling along the icy slope beneath which the immense bleeding animal stood motionlessly.

Suddenly Wamedee leaped astride the back of the wounded

buffalo. At exactly the same moment, Wabeda became so excited that he began to bark hysterically.

The buffalo bolted. Wamedee's knife fell to the ground, but somehow he managed to hang onto the long shaggy hair, staying precariously balanced on the bounding animal's back.

There was no chance to jump off. He had to remain in an impossible position on the buffalo's hump, where he was tossed and bounced with every movement of the enraged beast's body.

"Hurry! Hurry! Shoot! Shoot!" he shouted as the creature plunged and kicked madly in the deep snow.

Wamedee's face turned pale and he began to scream. To make matters worse, Wabeda broke away from Yesa and flew into the legs of the frantic buffalo, agitating the wounded animal to even greater excitement. And though Wamedee's friends pitied him they could not help laughing at the sight of the great hunter bounding through the deep snow on the back of a crazed buffalo.

"Shoot! Hurry! Please hurry and shoot!" Wamedee begged.

But no sooner did his friends take aim than he would suddenly cry: "Don't shoot! Don't shoot! You're sure to kill me!"

At last the exhausted animal fell down and died. And as Wamedee crawled out from under the lifeless buffalo, he turned glum with embarrassment. His friends could not resist tumbling into the snow, where they rolled with laughter.

From that day poor Wamedee was ridiculed by his people as a coward and a fool.

The fire had burned low, so Yesa pushed the embers together and wrapped his robe closely about his shoulders. There was a thunderous roar as the ice on the lake burst. Except for this occasional bombardment of sound the lodge was quiet. Uncheedah was restringing an old snowshoe.

Wabeda whined softly at the entrance and crept into the warmth of the lodge, bringing a large bone with him. But Uncheedah immediately drove him away. Though the dog always insisted upon bringing a bone into the tipi, Uncheedah was equally determined that the greasy, foul-smelling trophy be left outdoors.

"Uncheedah," Yesa pleaded, "pity Wabeda. If he buries the bone on the snow then *Shunktokecha*—the wolf—will surely steal it. Wabeda is always very anxious about his bones. And this one is especially fat and good."

"Either he leaves the bone outside," Uncheedah muttered resolutely, "or he stays outside with it!"

Wabeda looked beseechingly into his master's eyes, and lingered in the lodge entrance, anxiously wagging his big yellow tail.

"Come along, Wabeda," Yesa said, "let us bury your bone very carefully so that no *Shunktokecha* will take it."

The dog seemed delighted with the suggestion and followed Yesa into the freezing night.

They both dug in the snow and buried the bone very, very deep, first wrapping it in a piece of old, partially burned blanket, since Yesa knew that the wolf would not touch anything that was burned. Then they carefully covered the bone with snow.

For a moment Wabeda lingered over his treasure, unwilling to follow his master back into the warmth of the lodge. But after sniffing the air repeatedly and making a wide circle around the buried bone, he seemed satisfied that it was safe, and he came back to the tipi.

Uncheedah grunted as the dog appeared in the entrance blinking his large eyes. He awaited her invitation to sit by the fire. For a moment Uncheedah only nodded disapprovingly at the big yellow animal, but then Wabeda saw the glimmer of a smile on Grandmother's lips, and immediately his tail began to wag. Happily he entered the lodge and settled himself beside Yesa, and began nuzzling the warm furs beside the fire. Soon his eyes were closed and he puffed contentedly through his sagging black lips.

"Yesa, *coowah!*" came the call of Uncheedah.

The boy and his yellow dog came quickly out of the woods, where they had been watching the mice building a nest among the gnarled roots of a dead aspen.

When Yesa hastened into the lodge from which he had been summoned, he found his cousin, Oesedah, and her old mother, Wahchewin, sitting by the fire with his grandmother.

He greeted the guests with proper ceremony, and then he gazed for a long time at Oesedah, for she had become so beautiful that he hardly recognized the fragile turnip with whom he had spent so much time.

"You look well, Oesedah," he said, embarrassed for having stared at her.

Instantly his pretty cousin jumped up and embraced him, weeping with delight in seeing him. Despite her great physical beauty, she was still a child, and she hugged Yesa as if they were still playmates. There was something in her embrace so innocent that it astonished the young man, who quickly withdrew from her and nodded formally lest her mother, Wahchewin, take exception to his familiarity.

"Yes, you look well, Oesedah," he repeated.

The two old women took no notice of the embrace, but looked intently at Yesa, as if they had something of great importance to tell him. He sensed the seriousness of the situation and bowed to the women, taking a seat next to his grandmother.

"There is something that has been very difficult for me," Uncheedah said slowly. "It is the matter of assisting you in making your first personal offering to the Great Mystery."

Then Uncheedah was silent for a long time, as if she were deep in thought.

She was a holy woman, greatly concerned with the spiritual life of her people and her family. It had been her custom over many years to help each of her sons make his first sacrifice. Though many parents awaited the maturity of their children before initiating them into this serious practice, it had been Uncheedah's belief that truly powerful children should make their offering before their eighth summer. Yesa had almost reached his sixteenth summer, and still his grandmother hesitated to instruct him in making an offering. He was a young man of great sensitivity, filled with reverence for all creatures and love of the deep woods. Since Chatanna had been taken away from him, Yesa had spent much of his time in a spiritual solitude that awed the elders and won the respect of young men his own age. He was so gentle and wise for his age that his grandmother was reluctant to bring sorrow and sacrifice into his life. Already he had known much sadness. He had been motherless almost from the day of his birth. His father and eldest brothers had been murdered by the white men. And his dearest brother had been taken from him. But, despite these many painful experiences, Uncheedah knew that her grandson must make his first offering if he was to grow into a holy person with the power to heal the sick and give good words of counsel to those who sought his advice. And so she had asked Wahchewin to assist in Yesa's first offering to the Great Mystery.

Already it was whispered through the encampment that Uncheedah intended to give a feast to honor her grandchild's first sacrificial act. Even Oesedah had heard the good news. But as far as Uncheedah was concerned all this gossip was just idle talk, for the wise old grandmother was determined to keep the event a secret until the offering was completed, believing that the Great Mystery must always be met in silence and dignity, without fanfare or bragging.

Now Yesa sat silently beside his grandmother, his dog

Wabeda sprawled faithfully at his side, but the old woman could not bring herself to the subject she wanted most to discuss with her grandson.

"I have something to say to you," Uncheedah began slowly. "You see that you are now a man. It will not be long before you will leave me, for a warrior must seek opportunities to make him great among his people."

Yesa frowned at the idea of leaving his grandmother, and he glanced uncertainly at his cousin, whose expression was as striken by this news as his own, for they both feared that Uncheedah was preparing to give Yesa away as Mysterious Medicine had given Chatanna to the white trader.

"You must try to be as great as your father and grandfather," Uncheedah said. "They were warriors and feastmakers. But it is not the poor hunter who makes the feasts, my son. It is the warrior and the holy man who are blessed with an abundance of courage and wisdom by the Great Mystery. These are the gifts of the Great Mystery. And so it is, my son, that today you will make your first offering to him."

This news greatly excited Yesa and Oesedah, for both of them felt that an important event was about to take place.

After conferring briefly with Wahchewin, whose knowledge in such matters was very great, Uncheedah looked solemnly at her grandson and said: "You must give up one of your belongings. Whatsoever is dearest to you, that is what you must give as your sacrificial offering."

This command confused Yesa, for he was uncertain that he possessed anything valuable enough to be worthy of the Great Mystery. "I can give up my bear's claw necklace! And the rifle that Uncle gave to me. I can give up my bow and arrows and all the paints I have!" Yesa exclaimed proudly.

"Are these the things dearest to you?" Uncheedah demanded with a look of concern coming into her face.

"Not my bow and arrows. I admit that they are not precious. But my new rifle and the paints—they are certainly very dear to me because there are no traders in our region, and they would be very hard to replace. But," Yesa offered in the hope of proving himself unselfish in the presence of Oesedah, "I will also give up my otterskin headdress, if you think that what I have offered is not enough."

"Ai," Uncheedah sighed, ". . . try to think, my boy, for you have not yet mentioned the thing that you love the most and that would therefore be a fine offering to the Great Mystery."

Yesa looked into the old woman's face, but he could discover no hint of what she wanted him to say. He glanced at Wahchewin and then back at Uncheedah, but still he could not guess what great sacrifice the two old women wanted from him.

"I have nothing else as good as the things I have already named, Grandmother," he said slowly, ". . . unless you mean my spotted pony . . . and I am certain that the Great Mystery would not require a young man to make such a difficult sacrifice!"

The old women remained silent.

"Besides," Yesa objected, "that pony cost Mysterious Medicine three otterskins and five eagle feathers, and I promised him that I would keep my horse safe and away from the Blackfeet, who would steal him!"

"You must remember," Uncheedah said, "that in this offering you will call upon him who looks at you through the eyes of every creature upon the earth. In the wind you hear him whisper to you. He is the eagle and the smallest bird. He gives his war whoop in the thunder. And he watches you by day with his golden eye, which is the Sun; and with his silver eye, which is the Moon. It is to this ultimate Mystery that you will make your first offering. By this single act you will ask him to grant to you what he has granted to few men. I know you wish to be a great warrior and a holy man with vast knowledge. Such a man must have courage. If you are not willing to risk everything for your dream then you should decide now to be contented with an ordinary life among ordinary men. But if you wish to be favored with what few people are granted, then you can show no cowardice in your decisions and actions!''

During Uncheedah's speech, the young man glanced uncomfortably at Oesedah. In her sorrowful eyes he suddenly saw what sacrifice his grandmother wished for him to offer the Great Mystery. What he saw in his cousin's face so grieved Yesa that for a moment he could not think or speak.

It was very difficult for Uncheedah to tell her grandson that he must part with his dog, Wabeda. She might have failed to be equal to the situation had Yesa not slowly realized what Uncheedah could not bring herself to tell him.

Suddenly Oesedah sobbed and covered her face. The sound was so painful and remorseful that it was all Yesa could do not to weep. He swallowed hard and tried to look straight into his grandmother's solemn eyes.

"Yesa," she said very softly, "you are young and loving, but I know that you are also strong and courageous. I know that you will be willing to give up the very dearest things you have for your first offering. And so, child, you must give up Wabeda. He too is brave, and he will understand that you are honoring him with your sacrifice."

For a long time no one spoke. Oesedah's sobs quickly subsided and a terrible silence overcame the lodge.

"Come," Uncheedah said at length, ". . . here are four bundles of paints and a filled pipe. Let us go to the place of the sacrifice."

At first, Yesa did not seem to hear these last words. He did not move, nor did he say anything.

It was Oesedah who came to the young man's aid. "He is brave," she said in a firm voice, "but he is also full of love for the precious things the Great Mystery has made. It is not selfishness that makes this offering so difficult, but love for the good friendship of his dog!"

Yesa looked up at his cousin with deep appreciation in his eyes, and then turned to his grandmother. "Wabeda will have to die. Let me tie together the tails of two red squirrels and put them on his neck so the Great Mystery will know what a fine hunter he has been. Let me paint him by myself. Let me do all of this so he knows that I love him."

Uncheedah granted these requests, and then left with Wahche-win to ask Mysterious Medicine to execute the faithful dog.

Yesa began to sing a dirge for Wabeda, while he hugged him tightly and tried not to weep. "Be brave, Wabeda," he whispered. "I shall remember you the first time I go on the warpath against the white men who murdered my father."

Then Yesa quickly took out his paints and prepared Wabeda for death, painting his yellow body red and black. Then he carefully took a piece of red cloth and tied it around the dog's neck. To this cloth he fastened two squirrels' tails as well as a wing from the oriole that Chatanna had given him.

While Oesedah looked on with a pale, unmoving face, Yesa loosened his thick black braids and let his long hair hang down on his shoulders in mourning. Then he ground a charcoal and, mixing it with bear's oil, rubbed it on his face.

During this mournful preparation Uncheedah watched her grandson from the entrance of the lodge. She'd come very near withdrawing her command, but feared the misfortune she might call down upon Yesa should she falter and say: "Keep your dear dog! Keep him!"

Yesa now came out of the lodge with his black face looking like an eclipsed moon, leading his beautiful dog, who was handsomer than ever with the red designs painted upon his yellow body.

It was Uncheedah's turn to struggle with the storm of tears that burdened her. But the young man was encouraged by the people's admiration for his bravery as he and his dog walked through the encampment, surrounded by whispering men and women.

As soon as Uncheedah was able to speak, the loving grandmother murmured: "No, my young brave, it is not permitted for you to mourn for your first offering. Go to the creek and wash the charcoal from your face, and then we will go."

Yesa silently obeyed. He left his precious dog with Mysterious Medicine and walked off with his grandmother and Wahchewin.

Oesedah watched after her handsome cousin with tears in her eyes. For a moment she tried not to cry, but when Wabeda began to whimper for his departed master, she could not endure the sorrow. Quickly she ran to the river and buried her face among the thick, green leafy boughs of the willows.

Yesa and the two old women followed the footpath leading along the bank of the river, through a beautiful grove of oaks, and finally around and under a very high cliff. The murmuring of the river came up to them. On the opposite side of the wide stream was a white cliff from which extended a gradual slope of majestic trees. The young man was amazed by the intensity of the landscape, the brightness of the light, the greenness of the trees, and the fullness of every sound.

Wahchewin paused when the little party reached the edge of the cliff. It had already been arranged that she would wait there for Mysterious Medicine, who was to bring to the cliff the offering with which he had been entrusted.

The young man and his grandmother descended the steep bank, following a tortuous footpath, until they finally reached the water's edge. There they proceeded to the mouth of an immense black cave that hovered in the cliff above the rushing water.

A sense of wonder overcame Yesa as he entered the sweet-smelling cavern. It was surely the home of the Great Mystery, and the beauty of the vast, dark shrine helped him forget his sorrow.

Now Wahchewin came feebly up the path, carrying the body of Wabeda across her arms. At first Yesa could not bring himself to look at his dog. "Ai," he murmured as he stared into the darkness.

Then Wahchewin placed the body upon the ground and quickly departed.

As soon as the old woman had disappeared from view, Uncheedah unfastened the leather strings that held the four small bundles of paints and tobacco. Then she solemnly laid the filled pipe beside the dead Wabeda.

In the silence of that immense black cave she scattered paints and tobacco on the sacred ground. The old woman drew a deep breath and began to intone in an echoing whisper her prayer to the Great Mystery.

"O, Great Mystery, we hear your voice in the rushing water below us! We hear your whisper in the great oaks of these mountains! Our spirits are refreshed with your life-giving breathing that fills this cave. O, hear our prayer! Behold this young man and bless his life! Make him strong and wise as you also made his father and his grandfather before him!"

With this prayer the tears finally leaped into the grandmother's eyes, and she knelt on the earth, gazing at the body of Wabeda, while Yesa opened his mouth and shouted out a long, desperate cry of victory.

For a moment he saw the Moon hanging massive and heavy in the darkness of the cave, but then it vanished, and with it died the last fragile innocence of his childhood. In some strange and inexplicable way he had been transformed by the greatness of his sacrifice. And now something new and powerful filled his heart.

# Part Four

# In Quest of Vision

# Part Four

# In Quest of Vision

# FRIENDS

The summer was full of bees and the scent of blossoms. Yesa and his friends sat in the lodge, where the flaps had been rolled up to let the breeze sweep through their stifling dwelling. The air was good, and the young men sat back contentedly, watching the girls of Fort Ellis.

Mysterious Medicine had invited Yesa to accompany him to the Hudson Bay Company at the fort in Canada where the northern tribes had come for many years to replenish their gunpowder horns in exchange for pelts. Such a journey was an event of great importance to the young man, for he had never visited Manitoba, a remarkable place where there were many white people, half-breeds, and Indians from the various tribes.

"Yes," Uncheedah told her grandson as she watched him prepare to depart, "it will be a great adventure for you, but it will also be a sacred journey to a region where ten summers ago your poor father was killed by the soldiers."

Mourning for his father did not preoccupy Yesa as much as the excitement of taking an extraordinary trip. He was also pleased that the small caravan of horses loaded with skins included two young men who were his close friends.

Now these good companions, Redhorn and Tatanka, were

sitting with Yesa in their breeze-swept lodge, watching the girls go by.

"I have never seen so many people!" Redhorn admitted freely.

"Nor have I!" Tatanka agreed.

Yesa's eyes glowed as he gazed across the encampment. The old trading post of Fort Ellis stood on a vast tableland. Just behind the post and a full thousand feet above the Assiniboine River, surrounded completely by thick groves, there was a natural clearing, at the end of which stood the wooden fort. In this marvelous camp grounds there was a reunion of all the renegade bands of Yesa's tribe, as well as an assembly of the Assiniboines and Crees and various other Canadian tribes. Though it was an annual encampment, the arrangements were informal and friendly.

The Hudson Bay Company always had a good supply of red, blue, green, and white blankets, and by the time the trading was over all the Indians had brightly colored garments, which they wore with great pride. Paints of many brilliant colors could be bought. The Canadian Indian women wore buckskin dresses with short sleeves and decorations of beads and porcupine quills.

The three young men looked out into the sun-filled camp and were dazzled by the motion and color and beauty of all the people.

While Redhorn, Tatanka, and Yesa began eating their morning meal of buffalo jerky, Mysterious Medicine visited the trading post in order to finalize an excellent exchange with the shrewd white traders. And as the young men admired the girls passing by their lodge, they heard the voice of a crier galloping through the camp on his calico pony.

"White Eagle's daughter, the maiden Red Star, welcomes all the maidens of the tribes to come to her feast. It will be in the camp of her father, before the sun reaches the middle of the sky.

All true and virtuous girls are invited. Red Star also invites the young men to be present to see that no unworthy maiden should be admitted to the feast!''

This news sent a wave of exuberance throughout the camp. Tatanka, Redhorn, and Yesa gave forth loud whoops, and many of the other young men followed their example, until the entire camp was filled with shouts.

No sooner had the crier finished his rounds than the girls began to gather in great numbers. The fort was in a state of enormous jubilation, with laughter and merriment everywhere. Yet, despite the mood of celebration, the Maiden's Feast was a sacred event, and it was a desecration for any girl to attend who was not perfectly virtuous. Therefore the feast was an ideal opportunity for all the young, unmarried braves to discover which of the girls among the tribes were truly honorable. It was permitted for any man to challenge the virtue of any of the attending maidens. But woe to him who attempted to disgrace a woman without proof. His punishment would be severe.

From the hundreds of lodges the girls now came singly and in groups, dressed in bright calicoes or heavily fringed and elaborately beaded buckskin. Their cheeks and the crowns of their heads were touched with vermilion powder. Their smiles were glorious, and Yesa peered at them with delight. Every girl carried her own wooden bowl from which to eat at the feast. Some came from such a distance that they arrived on their ponies.

The maidens' circle was formed around a large rock that was painted red. Beside this rock two new arrows were stuck into the ground. This formed an altar, which each girl confronted with an oath before taking her place in the large circle, touching first the stone and then the arrows. By this gesture her oath of purity was declared. As each girl approached the altar there was a stir among the male spectators, and sometimes a young man would call out: "Take care! You will overturn the rock!"

Everyone laughed, for such a remark invariably made the girl nervous, but also amused the crowd.

Soon the area around the Maiden's Feast was overflowing. There had never been such a gorgeous and vast assembly at Fort Ellis. The Crees, displaying their exceptional horsemanship, pranced in circles on their handsome mounts; the Assiniboines, with their curious pompadours covered with red paint, mingled in the crowd. Everyone was wearing his or her most elegant regalia. And there were even a few white daughters of the trading post watching the events from a cautious distance.

Yesa had never before seen a white woman, and he could not help staring at their blonde hair and creamy skin. They looked to him like daughters of the Moon. From the distance they appeared to be made of silver, glistening in the sunlight.

Turning his attention back to the circle, he noticed more and more lovely maidens come shyly into the circle. It was an exciting sight. But suddenly there was a stir of anger in the crowd, and all the girls anxiously glanced toward the cause of the disturbance.

A tall youth emerged from the throng of spectators and advanced toward the circle as everyone glared at him in the hope of deterring him from his intentions. He would not be put off. With a steady step he passed through the crowd of young men who attempted to stop him, and took his place behind a very pretty Assiniboine maiden. Loudly, he called out: "I am sorry, my friends, but according to custom this girl should not be here!"

A wave of outrage swept through the crowd as Yesa and his two friends attempted to squeeze through the people and get closer to the disturbance.

The Assiniboine girl trembled with confusion and embarrassment, but soon she recovered her composure and angrily faced the young man who had accused her.

"What are you saying?" she demanded indignantly. "Three times you have come to court me, but each time I have refused to listen to you. And now you try to disgrace me!"

There were angry shouts in the crowd, and the young man visibly backed away as the girl continued: "I turned my back upon you. Twice I was with Mashtinna. She can tell the people that all I say is true. The third time I had gone for water when you stopped me and begged me to listen to your passionate speeches. But I refused because I did not know you. My chaperon, Makatopawee, knows that I was away from the lodge for only a brief time. She can tell the people that what I say is true. I never spoke to you and I never accepted your courtship!"

The young man stammered, unable to answer the girl's retort. The people became very angry, as it seemed clear that the youth had sought to avenge himself upon the girl in return for her lack of interest in him.

"Carry him out!" was the order of the chief of the Indian police who supervised the feast. "Take him away and chastise him well so he will not speak falsely against a maiden again!"

The audacious young man was hurried away into the ravine, where he was beaten and shamed. His cries of pain echoed back into the circle, where the maidens' song was sung and four times the girls danced in a ring around the altar. Then the feast was served, after which each girl once more made an oath to remain a virgin until she took a husband.

These events roused the ardor and restlessness of the young braves of the vast encampment. Though the assembled tribes were friendly, there was much talk and boasting of horse raids and tribal wars. At just such moments there were always many holy men in readiness. Their vocation was to see into the future, and each was willing to make medicine for any young man who was impatient for the warpath. Inevitably those who were anxious for war received a prophecy that favored their immediate departure for enemy territory.

The young men of Yesa's band received such a sign of war, and for a few days there was great excitement and many preparations for hostilities. On the appointed morning of the raid, Yesa, Redhorn, and Tatanka were awakened by the songs of the warriors and the wailing of the women.

"You will stay," Mysterious Medicine commanded when his sunrise prayers were disturbed by the war songs. "Such an undertaking is foolish. The country in which they will be roaming is not our own and they are likely at any time to be captured for trespassing by the rightful people of the land. Let the hotheads go!" he shouted angrily. "If old Hotanka or Loud-Voiced Raven wishes to lead such a bunch of boys on a raid, let them so do! But the three of you are in my charge and you will remain here with me until it is time to return to the lodges of your grandmothers!"

"Uncle," Yesa asked eagerly, "must we stay? Will you not join the raid on the Gros Ventres?"

"No," he replied with a long sigh. "I do not need to prove my courage like a colt! It is the worst time of the year to go on the warpath. We shall have plenty of fighting when we return south and must confront our enemies, the Ojibwa!"

The war drums continued throughout the day, and all the young men worked themselves into the frenzy of excitement. Most of them had never been on a raid, and their nervousness and eagerness ignited into a flamboyant show of courage that both amused and alarmed the older men.

By now it was evening. The war drum was answered by the howls of coyotes on the opposite side of the river. Yesa, Tatanka, and Redhorn wandered among the throngs of men who were preparing for glory.

"I wish we could go with them!" Redhorn said earnestly. "I

wish we were old enough so we could go where we liked! I would stop at nothing to go with this raiding party!"

"Then why don't you go?" Tatanka whispered.

"What are you saying?" Yesa exclaimed. "It is forbidden until you are married!"

"I am older than either of you," Tatanka said confidently. "And Mysterious Medicine is not *my* uncle! When morning comes I will go with the braves."

Suddenly Tatanka pulled away from Yesa's grasp and hurried into the circle of dancing warriors. Redhorn was about to follow after him, but Yesa said, "My friend, do not be foolish. This is not a good time for us to go to war. We must obey my uncle."

Redhorn was momentarily captivated by Yesa's logic, and he paused just long enough for the impulse within him to fade. He sighed despondently as he remained standing with Yesa. Now both the young friends looked out into the blazing dance circle, where Tatanka leaped and stomped with the other braves until the Moon was pale and the dawn made its way into the sky.

Then, as the women wailed, the young men rode out of camp shouting great war whoops with a splendid flourish of pride.

All was now quiet. But gradually, at a very great distance, Yesa could hear the sounds of battle. At first they were very far away, but then they seemed closer and closer. The women of the camp appeared to grow more and more calm. Everyone waited.

It seemed that an eternity had passed, when suddenly a tremendous burst of whoops thundered through the tablelands. The mothers of the youths who had gone on the warpath waited anxiously, their faces still filled with a terrible calm.

*Silence.* The retreating roar of horses and then vast silence.

After a very long time, when it was already evening, the long and solitary song of a single brave was heard. In an instant the camp was thrown into utter confusion. The meaning of that sad song was clear to everyone—all but one member of the war party was dead. The survivor's lone and mournful song announced the fate of all his comrades.

Tatanka had been killed. An arrow had pierced his heart and he had fallen from his horse. Nothing remained of the young Indian but his headdress and his blood-splattered mare.

Yesa and Redhorn tried to console each other, but the loss of their companion of many hunts, games, and contests was so great a calamity that they could not speak of it.

Yesa took one of Tatanka's eagle feathers, promising faithfully to wear it on the first day that he went on the warpath. All of his life Yesa had been taught to loathe the white men for murdering his father and brothers, but only now did he fully realize how capable he was of hatred. Now, however, it was not the white man he hated. It was the Gros Ventres, who had killed his cherished friend.

The war songs, the endless wailing for the dead, and the howling of the dogs filled the night. Yesa could not bear the agony of his people.

Finally a terrible silence descended upon the wide tableland around Fort Ellis. In the morning the tribes broke camp, and Mysterious Medicine, Redhorn, and Yesa departed silently for the distant lodge of Uncheedah. Trailing behind Yesa's pony was the handsome horse on which Tatanka had ridden off to war. Nothing more remained of the proud young man who had given up his life on his first day of battle.

# BEAR DANCE

Turtle Mountain was dressed in a thick robe of crystals and snow. The evening was blue and cold. It was Yesa's sixteenth winter, and he had grown tall and strong. Under the close supervision of Mysterious Medicine his body had become firm and agile due to the many fasts and early morning swims in the icy lakes. And Uncheedah's teachings had educated him in the many days of his people, in their sacred memories, and in their rituals. He had been given a warm heart by his grandmother, and in the evening he still clung closely to the edge of the dark woods where he could talk to the birds and animals.

A short distance from the camp beside this same forest there was a village made of loghouses. It was the home of the French Canadian half-breeds. They were a peculiar people, and Yesa's tribe was so distrustful of them that the two camps never intermingled.

But this seclusion did not last long.

One night in the very early hours of morning there was a sudden volley of countless gunshots. Instantly Mysterious Medicine and Yesa leaped from their couches, fully alert and ready for any kind of danger. With rifles in hand they cautiously crept from their lodge and joined the other men in the shadows. There they discussed the barrage of shots that had awakened the encampment.

Some of the men speculated that the trouble was at the half-breeds' village.

"Maybe they've been attacked!" Redhorn exclaimed as he clutched his rifle to his chest, ready at any moment to ward off an ambush by the Gros Ventres.

"Ai!" Mysterious Medicine shouted as another volley of explosions thundered in the distance. "There it is again!"

It was decided that the half-breeds were probably under attack, and if so it was the duty of the tribe to assist them, since they were helpless people who had never offended anybody.

Without wasting another moment, all the men saddled their horses and prepared to leave for the loghouse village.

Uncheedah came solemnly from the lodge and gazed at Yesa as he mounted his gallant pony. This would be the young man's first battle, and the grandmother wanted to send all of her silent prayers with him. But before she could open her heart in a long wail of farewell, Redhorn rode up to Yesa's side, and with a resounding whoop, the two friends lurched into the darkness and galloped away.

They flew through the darkness with the cold wind gusting into their faces. They knew every knoll and tree of the landscape, and with the aid of the blazing moon, which lighted the valley and the woods, they made their way across the snowy ground. In the distance old Turtle Mountain presided over the glorious, luminous land, his monumental head held high in a headdress of stars.

Redhorn and Yesa had trained their whole lives for this moment. They had often talked about such a battle and had practiced many cunning maneuvers in mock wars with their companions. Now all they had dreamed about and all that they had learned was to be put to the test.

They rode close to each other, Redhorn slightly ahead, so they could quickly come to each other's aid, but not so close that they could be assaulted as a single target. They kept their eyes trained upon the wide landscape, seeing into the distant shadows, ready to react should there be the slightest movement, the slightest sign of danger.

Again there was a great barrage of gunshots and much shouting. They were close to the log house village now, and everyone could hear the frantic cries of the women and the galloping and snorting of many horses. Another burst of fire! Now the exchange of shots had become a full-scale battle. And as the men saw the bonfires and the struggling, running, leaping shadows of the villagers through the trees, they feared that perhaps they would be greatly outnumbered by the Gros Ventres.

Mysterious Medicine turned to his young braves with a determined gleam in his eyes and issued a great, roaring war whoop to give the young men courage. Every brave responded with a colossal battle cry, and then together they dashed through the trees and broke out into the clearing of the half-breed village.

Yesa's heart filled his chest with a gust of energy as he burst from the woods into the flames and mad confusion.

"Ai! What is this?" Mysterious Medicine shouted angrily as he quickly drew up his horse, at first bewildered, and then annoyed.

The flames were only a bonfire. The people hectically prancing through the clearing were just drunken half-breed dancers. The countless gunshots were noises of celebration.

"Ai! What crazy people these half-breeds are!" the warriors grumbled in embarrassment, as they dismounted to the warm greetings of the uproarious revelers.

It seemed that all the commotion was the result of a white man's holiday that the French Canadian half-breeds were celebrating. It was the Moon of Difficulty, but to them it was December thirty-first, and it was at this time that they welcomed the birth of a new year!

Yesa and Redhorn looked speechlessly at each other with utter disappointment. There would be no battle!

Meanwhile all the men of the tribe were treated to *minnewakan* —the "spirit water" so popular among the whites and the half-breeds. And soon everyone was crazy and foolish. They wheeled and bragged and fought over trivial matters that were not worth the pride of a true warrior.

"Come," Redhorn urged his friend, "let us join the celebration!"

But Yesa did not want to drink the spirit water. He had seen men acting crazy and foolish because they had drunk *minnewakan*. He wanted no part of such festivities.

"Come, Yesa, my friend; all the young men are drinking the spirit water! Do you want us to be left out?"

"No," Yesa insisted. Redhorn shrugged, smiled widely, and ran off to join the others as they staggered and tumbled, laughing uncontrollably over everything.

The head chief, appalled by the indignities, finally ordered Yesa and several other sober braves to tie up those who were drunk and take them back to camp. He insisted they be put into a lodge by themselves so they would not disturb the rest of the tribe.

But the drunk men shouted and laughed all night, begging to be untied, and for more spirit water. The chief remained firm, however, and gave orders not to untie any of them until the evil spirit had left their bodies.

During the next day all the people of Yesa's tribe were invited to attend the half-breeds' dance. And having never seen the way the whites did their dances, Yesa and Redhorn gladly accepted the invitation.

The ceremony took place in a loghouse in the middle of the

half-breed village. The house was completely filled with people,
so many men and women in fact that Redhorn and Yesa had to
stand outside and glimpse the strange ritual by looking through
one of the holes that was cut in the wall of the cabin to let in the
daylight.

Yesa peered inside the crowded house and was astonished to
see a man sitting in a corner, sawing away at a board with many
strings stretched over it. It made the most terrible, screeching
sound he had ever heard. But the half-breeds seemed to like the
noise, for they were all stamping the floor with their feet and
laughing with one another.

Every time the man shouted out something in the language of
the French Canadians, the dancers suddenly stopped doing what
they had been doing, and immediately began all sorts of different
antics: spinning, skipping, jumping, and moving in every con-
ceivable unruly manner.

For Redhorn and Yesa the most startling discovery was to see
the men dancing with women. When the elder with the string-
board shouted, the men abruptly swung the women around and
around, as if they were trying to make them fall down. Their
antics looked very rude to the two young friends, and they stared
in astonishment at the dancing couples, who pranced and stepped
so fast that they would surely wear out their mocassins against the
rough floorboards!

Then an old man with long curly hair and a foxskin cap
perched on his shaggy head began to dance all by himself in the
middle of the cabin, violently slapping the floor with his feet. He
seemed to be a leader among his people, and therefore when he
invited the chiefs of Yesa's tribe to join him, they were reluctant
to insult the half-breeds by refusing. One of the warriors politely
came to the center of the crowd and held himself very elegantly
as he performed an ancient dance.

The half-breeds seemed to enjoy his performance, for they

cheered and smiled brightly. Then the young warriors gave a great war whoop while the half-breed leader and the Indian who had danced drank together. After this, there was so much drinking and loud talking among the men that it was finally decided to send the young men back to the camp.

Mysterious Medicine looked at Yesa disapprovingly when he and Redhorn objected to leaving.

"It is the decision of the elders!" the uncle said very sternly. "And you will obey whatever you are told. So go back to your grandmother at once and be glad that you are not one of these foolish braggarts who is making noise like the thunder and forgetting that he is the son of a noble father!"

Yesa would have argued with his uncle, for he was now a man and he objected to being sent away like a child, but Redhorn had been feeling very weak for many days and this night his nose had suddenly begun to bleed.

Nodding humbly to Mysterious Medicine, Yesa turned to Redhorn and helped him to his horse. The young man's energy was gone and he could not ride by himself. Yesa embraced his friend with great compassion and concern, taking him onto his own saddle where he could hold him securely as they rode double, with Redhorn's pony following directly behind them.

As they rode slowly through the icy night, Redhorn began to cough and blood poured from his mouth. He shook with convulsions until he collapsed, and Yesa had to lash his friend to his own body in order to keep him mounted.

When they arrived at the camp, Redhorn's mother hurried to meet them, having awakened from a dream that told her her son was gravely ill.

The next morning when Yesa went to visit his friend, he found him pale and weak, unable to rise, and barely able to speak.

"Redhorn . . . I have had no sleep. All night I sat by the fire and thought about you. I prayed that I would find you recovered."

"No . . ." Redhorn gasped in a fragile voice. "It is not good with me. But my grandmother is a wise woman and she has discovered the cause of my illness."

Yesa was much relieved. "And can she cure you?" he exclaimed.

"Of course," Redhorn whispered as he tried to smile. "But she cannot do so until I have fulfilled the commandment."

"Ai . . ." Yesa murmured, "what is the commandment, my friend? What commandment must you fulfill?"

Redhorn nodded in shame and did not speak for a moment. He turned away, for he could not look at Yesa. "I have confessed to my grandmother," he whispered, "that two winters ago I received my commission and I should have made a Bear Dance and proclaimed myself a medicine man."

Redhorn was silent a moment, then continued.

"What I have done," he muttered sadly, "is surely very wrong. I was given a great vision when I was but thirteen winters. I should have rejoiced, but I was too ashamed to proclaim myself a medicine man, for I was young and I thought the men would ridicule me."

Redhorn searched Yesa's face, desperately looking for some sign of sympathy. "I know what I have done is wrong," he said, "and I know that it is for this reason that I am punished with this terrible sickness. But I was young and I was afraid of the powerful vision that came to me in the woods!"

Yesa could not speak. He was so confused that he could not think of anything to say. He was overwhelmed with envy for Redhorn and was deeply ashamed of himself. He had so often hoped for some great animal to appear to him in a vision and give him the secret commission that provided only the most important of people with a glorious purpose in their lives. No such commandment had ever been given Yesa. He was both grief-stricken for Redhorn and torn by his own longings. Yesa bit his lip, and took his friend's hand.

"My grandmother says that it is still not too late for me," Redhorn sighed. "She says that I can still carry out my commandment. But Yesa! . . . I am so weak now! I can scarcely stand up! I am no longer afraid to fulfill my commandment, but I do not know if I have the strength to do so!"

Redhorn began to cough again, and Yesa looked on with deepening fear for his friend's life as the blood trickled from his mouth and his eyes filled with pain.

The grandmothers at that moment hurried to the stricken young man and hunched over his body, wringing their hands and wailing.

There was a great silence now. Yesa held his breath and peered down at his friend, praying that he would open his eyes, that he would speak and live and grow strong so they could again go on the warpath together!

"Ai . . ." Redhorn murmured so softly that Yesa had to come closer to hear his words. "My grandmother," he panted with great effort, ". . . my grandmother, she says . . . she says that I can appoint someone . . . someone else to act for me. That is what she says . . . that I can appoint someone to be the bear in the dance." With this Redhorn opened his eyes and tried to raise himself so he could whisper into Yesa's ear. "Ai . . . my friend," he gasped, ". . . Yesa, will you act in my behalf? Will you dance the bear for me?"

"Yes . . . yes . . . yes . . ." Yesa murmured anxiously.

"You know . . . you know the dance . . . the bear must chase the dancers . . . he must chase all the dancers away from his den," Redhorn murmured, and gradually lowered his head to the couch and closed his eyes again.

"Redhorn!" Yesa declared, getting up and wiping away his

tears. "I will do anything that will help you. But, my friend, how can I be the bear? I who have had no vision, no commandment? I am not fit for such an honor! I am not strong enough. I fear that the Great Mystery will not be pleased with me as your substitute!"

Redhorn did not open his eyes. In a frail voice he said, "You must do this for me, Yesa, or I will surely die."

After a very long silence, during which the grandmothers gazed hopefully at Yesa, he nodded uncertainly. "Yes," he said very quietly. "I will do it."

A few days later it was announced by the camp crier that Redhorn would give a Bear Dance at which he would be publicly proclaimed a holy man.

On the appointed day the den of the bear was carefully dug at a short distance from the camp. Redhorn, wrapped securely in a warm blanket, was placed by his grandmothers into this shallow hole. Though he could not perform the dance, he was required to remain in the den and join in the singing of the bear song.

An arbor of green boughs was constructed over the den, and then everyone withdrew and awaited the call to the dance.

At sunrise the bear man—Yesa—began to sing the song, and all the men and boys gathered and danced around his den. Yesa nodded to his sick friend, who was so weak he could only add the smallest voice to the sacred song.

Then suddenly a great determination seized Yesa and he closed his eyes and raised his voice.

"Watch out! Watch out for the bear!" the women shouted anxiously, for any dancer who felt the touch of the bear would surely die.

But to the dancers there was something worse.

What frightened them most was the chance that they might fall while pursued by the bear, for they also believed that should this happen, there would soon be a dreadful death in the family of whosoever fell down!

When an elder gave the sign, all the boys and men started for the bear's den, like a pack of dogs. Yesa pounded on the drum and sang the bear's song, which Redhorn's grandmother had carefully taught him. He was transformed by the rugged melody, and he felt strong and fierce as he hunched in his den and watched the dancers swooping down upon him. Frantically, they yelled and whooped, running around the arbor in hops, skips, and wide jumps.

"Now you are the bear!" Redhorn whispered in a strange voice, trembling and peering at his friend as if he had truly been transformed into the great grizzly. "Jump!" Redhorn exclaimed. "Run after them, bear man! Run!"

The bear lurched.

But a warrior gave a warning, and before Yesa could reach out and touch anyone, the dancers scattered as if they were running for their lives.

Then, gradually, the dancers slackened their pace and began to torment the bear man with switches. They cautiously whipped Yesa's naked body, and soon the attack was so painful that the bear man withdrew.

Now the dancers charged after him until he retreated into his den and growled confidently at Redhorn.

After a brief rest the tomtom and the song of the bear arose once again. Yesa huddled in his den and peered out at his tormentors. This time they began their attack upon the arbor less cautiously, and Yesa waited breathlessly for exactly the right moment to spring upon them unawares.

*Now!*

Out of the arbor he flew, grasping in every direction as he attempted to touch the fleeing, screaming dancers. He was overcome by power as he chased them, becoming so excited that he

roared. Gradually he overtook a man who had particularly enraged him with taunts. This man turned upon the bear and fired
his gun into the air, making a loathsome face. Yesa roared again
as the man slowly changed into a Gros Ventre. Yesa shuddered
with rage as he leaped toward this enemy who had insulted the
bear. Then, just as the man turned again to fire his rifle, a look
of horror suddenly filled his eyes. His feet became hopelessly
tangled as he attempted to run. He stumbled. He waved his
arms, trying to keep his balance. Then *crash!* . . . he fell to the
ground and the bear was instantly on top of him.

People began to scream in real panic. Everyone rushed away
in terror. The poor man who had fallen whimpered pathetically
and slowly crawled out from under Yesa, who was dazed from
exhaustion. The dancers gathered together in groups and exchanged desperate whispers.

"This is a great misfortune," they murmured.

"The man who fell . . . he is the most surefooted of us all!"

"Will he die? Will he die now?"

"Must his daughter die?"

The man did not speak for a very long time. He stood panting,
his head hung down. Finally he raised his voice and said: "We
all must die, and when the Great Mystery calls us we must obey
him, just as we would obey one of our own war chiefs here on
earth. I am not sad for myself, but my heart is not willing that
my firstborn daughter should be called."

No one replied. The camp was utterly silent. Drained, but
relieved, Yesa stumbled back to the bear's den to tell Redhorn
that his commandment was finally fulfilled. The Bear Dance was
over!

When he climbed down into the hole beneath the arbor he
looked happily into his friend's face. "Redhorn . . ." he murmured. But the young man could not answer. His mouth hung
open and in his eyes there was a vast darkness.

"Ai!" Yesa wailed. "He is dead! Redhorn, the bear man, he is dead!"

All the people rushed to the den and stared down at Yesa, who hugged his lifeless friend in his arms.

But even before the wailing for Redhorn had ended there was another commotion in the camp. The people ran toward the council lodge, where a holy man sadly announced that the man who had fallen during the dance was also dead.

Yesa sat desolate and fearful in the den of the bear man, staring at the vast and frantic expression of horror that still filled the face of his friend. Now the wind came up suddenly, tearing away the boughs of the arbor, spinning leaves and dust devils in the gray evening. When at last it was night, Yesa still clung to Redhorn, half buried in the wide, desolate prairie where shadows danced and the air was filled with the muffled roar of something strange and deadly that Yesa could not understand.

Part Five

# In the Land
# of the Dead

# RENEWAL

O esedah sat silently watching Yesa. She could no longer speak to him. A gray mood perpetually hung about his shoulders. He stared off into the air and only when someone tried to comfort him did he seem to awaken back into the world. A trace of feeling would pass momentarily through his eyes and then suddenly a savage misery would turn his features back into the face of an old man. It frightened Oesedah to watch her dear cousin withdrawing into a dream where she could not reach him. Every day he seemed to become more deeply lost in his terrible grief.

Uncheedah had prayed. She had given him herbs and she had begged the assistance of the holy men and women of the tribe. But nothing seemed to bring a smile back to Yesa's lips. Mysterious Medicine had talked softly to the young man, telling him that a warrior had to learn to leave lamentation behind him. But Yesa did not seem to hear his uncle's advice. For a very long time the young warrior sat idly in the lodge, without speaking or eating. Finally in desperation his uncle went in search of Matogee and invited this funny old man to visit Yesa.

Matogee was a peculiar fellow. Most of the time he was stern and silent, but now and again when the men urged him to tell some of his stories, he would wink an eye and begin to speak.

"Mysterious Medicine," he said quite seriously when he took the place of honor and greeted Uncheedah and Yesa, "I am very happy to accept your invitation, but I do not have any stories to tell Yesa. He looks so sour I am afraid he would throw me into the river if by chance I made him laugh!"

Mysterious Medicine smiled and Oesedah and Uncheedah expectantly looked into Yesa's face, hoping he too might be amused, but his eyes continued to stare off into the air.

This did not discourage old Matogee.

"Mysterious Medicine," he continued with a grin, "I heard that you tried to catch a buck by holding onto his tail."

Uncheedah giggled as Mysterious Medicine became very indignant and gestured for Matogee to be silent. "That is not why I asked you to visit my lodge," he muttered with annoyance. "I am tired of hearing that silly story! If you are going to talk to me then talk about something else!"

"Ai, my friend," Matogee laughed. "I will happily talk about something else. But, I must admit to you, I am sorry to hear that you really didn't try to catch a buck by the tail. It seemed to be a very good story!"

Mysterious Medicine grunted with exasperation, for he realized that Matogee was determined to ridicule him.

It was true that while hunting one day, he had only stunned a buck that he thought he had killed. When he approached the large animal, it suddenly leaped to its feet and attempted to escape. Mysterious Medicine frantically grabbed for the buck, but missed the legs and grasped the tail instead. Instantly he was pulled out into the meadow, where he ran behind the beast, holding the tail until it finally came off in his hands. Matogee enjoyed nothing better than recalling that embarrassing story.

"Yes," Mysterious Medicine replied. "I had to try to do something to outdo the story of the hunter who rode a young elk and yelled frantically for help the whole time he was on its back."

"Ai! But that is only a legend," retorted old Matogee, for he himself was the youthful unwilling hero of that tale. "But the story of your capturing the deer by the tail, my friend, that is the truth. I remember it very well. I could not tell which was more frightened—the buck or you. The deer's eyes were bulging out of their sockets while all the time your mouth was constantly enlarging from ear to ear. You cried out like a baby the whole time! That story will always be part of the tradition of our people," Matogee added, with a smile of satisfaction.

"Ah," Mysterious Medicine mused nostalgically. "It was certainly a singular disaster. I will admit to that!"

Now the pipe had been filled and passed to Mysterious Medicine good-naturedly, but Matogee still had a wide smirk on his face.

"It surely must be acknowledged," Matogee continued, "that you have a very strong grip, for no one else could have held onto a deer's tail as you did . . . and win such a splendid trophy besides."

Uncheedah and Oesedah could not resist smiling at Mysterious Medicine's mortification. But Yesa did not seem to hear the humorous thrashing his uncle was getting from sly old Matogee.

Several young men did hear the giggling, and they hurried into the lodge, suspecting that something very amusing was taking place. When they saw that Matogee was telling his outrageous stories, they called out to their friends to join them, and soon the lodge was crowded with onlookers.

"I think we should hear the whole tale," urged the latecomers.

The lodge was brightly lit by the burning coals, and all the people were sitting comfortably with their knees up against their chests. They waited expectantly for Matogee to tell the famous comedic tale of how Mysterious Medicine had tried to catch a buck by the tail.

"Well," Matogee said with a wide grin, "I am certainly willing

to tell you all about it, but I would not want to injure the feelings
of my old friend, Mysterious Medicine. So I am reluctant to
speak," the old man continued in a sarcastic tone of voice, "unless, of course, Mysterious Medicine does not mind my retelling
the tale."

Mysterious Medicine grunted as all the visitors mockingly
urged him to give his permission. "Uh . . . what nonsense this
is!" he growled. "Go ahead . . . go ahead and tell that foolish
story if it gives you such pleasure to ridicule me!"

Matogee thanked his friend and, with a very serious expression on his face, turned to his small audience. "This is exactly
what I saw. I was tracking a doe. As I approached a small opening
at the side of the creek there was a gunshot. *Boom!* Just like that!
Well, I decided that some great hunter was chasing a fine young
deer, so I remained quiet and stopped in the underbrush, hoping
to see a deer come leaping into the open meadow. Immediately
a fine buck dashed into the clearing with Mysterious Medicine
close behind him. I was astonished to discover that my then-
young friend, Mysterious Medicine, was holding onto the deer's
little tail with both hands. He had his knife in his teeth and he
was being pulled along so rapidly that the knife suddenly
dropped into the grass. At once he began to bellow at the deer
like a policeman, ordering it to stop!"

Everyone laughed. Oesedah and Uncheedah and even Mysterious Medicine broke into broad grins, but Yesa still sat silently,
staring into space.

"Well," Matogee continued, with his eyes lit up with gaiety,
"I shouted to Mysterious Medicine: 'My friend, haven't you got
hold of the wrong kind of animal?' But as I spoke the dashing
pair disappeared into the woods. In a moment they both reap-
peared. Then I really began to laugh. Just a little at first, because
I was greatly worried about the safety of my crazy friend, but
gradually as I watched Mysterious Medicine and that frantic deer

dash headlong across the meadow, I could not stop laughing. It very nearly killed me. The deer jumped the longest jumps I have ever seen. And here came Mysterious Medicine, hanging on for his life, running and falling and slipping and sliding and running some more—keeping pace with that buck! Well, by this time I was laughing so hard I was ready to fall down, when they again vanished into the woods like a streak of lightning. When they came out for the third time, it seemed as if the woods and the meadow were moving along with them. Everything was a blur. Mysterious Medicine skipped across the opening as if he were some kind of overgrown grasshopper learning to hop. Well, I just fell down flat. I couldn't stop laughing. And when I finally came to my senses, Mysterious Medicine was standing next to me gloomily shaking his head. 'Bad luck,' I told him while I tried not to laugh, 'he must have gotten away.' For a moment Mysterious Medicine looked down at me very unhappily. But then a boyish smile came over his face as he said, 'But I never lost my grip!' And he held up that buck's pathetic little tail!''

The people roared with laughter, and Mysterious Medicine himself heartily joined in the mirth. But when he looked at Yesa, he could see that the young man had not heard a word of the story.

Mysterious Medicine would not give up. If there was anyone in the world who could make someone laugh it was old Matogee, and so he said, "The strangest thing about that old mishap of mine is that I dreamed the whole thing the night before it happened."

"There are some dreams that come true," said one of the visitors. "I am a believer in dreams."

"Yes, certainly, so are we all," Matogee agreed. "Do you know that I knew a man named Hachah who very nearly lost his life because he believed in dreams?"

"Let us hear that story," everyone shouted eagerly.

The noise that filled the lodge momentarily caught Yesa's attention, and before he could slip back into his mournful reverie, Matogee made a funny gesture and began his story.

"You have perhaps heard of Hachah, the great medicine man, who did many wonderful things among our people many years ago. Well, he once dreamed four nights in succession of flying from a very high cliff over the Minnesota River. The dreams were so vivid that he could recall every detail of the scene. The day after having had the dream for the fourth time, he proposed to his wife that they go down to the river to swim. But, of course, his real purpose was to find the place where his dreams took place. At first he could not find it, and it seemed to Hachah that his dream was not as important as he had hoped it to be. Just when he was about to give up the search, he suddenly came upon a place on the river that was exactly the same in every detail as the place of his dreams. A crooked tree grew out of the top of the cliff over a bend in the deep, clear river."

Then Matogee was silent for a moment as he glanced at Yesa. At last the sad young man was alert and looking at the storyteller, waiting for him to continue his tale.

"Did he really fly?" Yesa asked.

"Ai, that is what I shall tell you," Matogee whispered with a grin of satisfaction. "Are you listening carefully? Are all of you listening to me? Well then, I shall tell you exactly what happened! Machah was swimming with his wife when all at once he seemed to vanish. His wife looked all around, calling to him everywhere. She finally spotted him standing way, way up on that cliff, clinging to the very tree that he had seen in his dreams!

"Well, Hachah looked out over the water, summoning all of his courage, because despite what he'd been taught he was sure that he could indeed fly. After a few moments he launched himself bravely into the air, sailing with his arms wide apart over the cliff. He gracefully kicked his little legs and he waved and flapped his arms very nicely, and for a moment he seemed to float like some large bird in the sky. But suddenly he plummeted down down down—and landed flat on the water like a crow shot in the wing!"

Everyone began to laugh. Everyone except Yesa, whose face remained as gloomy as before.

Matogee said, "Well, his wife screamed and screamed as he came tumbling from the sky, and when she saw him vanish into the water like a heron after a fish she feared he might drown, so she swam out to him and dragged him to the shore while he protested and sputtered. 'What are you trying to do, you fool?' she said to him. 'Do you want to get yourself killed?' she shouted again and again. Hachah did not say a word until he was back at his lodge sitting before a warm fire. Finally he glanced uncomfortably at his wife and said, 'Well, dreams can't be right every time!' And he did not tell anybody about his dreams for many years. Not until he was a very old man, and then Hachah told how one day in his youth he had thought he could fly."

At this everyone laughed harder than ever. Again Matogee expectantly looked at Yesa. The young man was grinning slightly. As the people laughed louder and louder, Yesa's grin broadened into a big smile and, finally, the gloom withered. Yesa's eyes lit up with merriment and he began to live again.

# LONG KNIVES

The tribe was camped on the Souris River. The buffalo were still plentiful and the bright summer days were good. It seemed a time free of troubles.

Then one afternoon a scout galloped into the camp and announced with alarm that United States troops were rapidly approaching. This report brought all the men and women out of their lodges. There was great uneasiness among the people.

A council was held immediately, and during that meeting the scout was put through a rigid cross-examination by the elders. Before a decision had been reached, another scout came in from the mountains. He claimed that his vantage from the heights had allowed him to see the valley more clearly than the other scout.

"These travelers, are not soldiers, but Canadian families. I could plainly see the dust raised by their carts," he insisted.

The two reports differed so greatly that the elders decided to send out more runners to observe this troop, in order to determine with certainty its purpose for being in the region.

Within a short time the swift scouts had returned and all the people waited anxiously for their report.

"They are not soldiers!" the scouts announced to the frightened people.

"They cannot be soldiers," another scout exclaimed, "for

there is no bright metal in the moving train to send off flashes of light that we could easily see, and no ranks of soldiers on horseback. There are only carts with ponies!"

After hearing these reports the tribe concluded that the on-coming caravan were the *bois brûlés*—the mixed-blood Indians of Canada.

Yesa and his grandmother sat anxiously in their lodge, await-ing the arrival of the French Cree, who spoke the peculiar lan-guage of the French fur traders, who were their fathers, but who had the faces of their Indian mothers. Mysterious Medicine re-mained with the elders in council, discussing a plan in the event the visitors became hostile.

While watching the sunset that evening Yesa suddenly looked up. His well-trained ears had picked up the peculiar music that accompanied a moving train of carts . . . a distant sound like the grunting and squealing of pigs. Instantly all the dogs of the camp began to bark uproariously, and soon no one could make them-selves heard over the mayhem.

The French Crees stopped a short distance from the camp, upon a gray plain, and turned their ponies in order to draw their clumsy carts into a circle. It formed a perfect, strong barricade, making it clear that the French-speaking Indians were aware they were invading another tribe's territory. Within this circle of carts the tipis were pitched, and soon many cheerful fires were kindled in the failing light of evening.

The chiefs of Yesa's people lost no time in appointing Mysteri-ous Medicine and two other warriors to ride out and meet with the strangers. They did so confidently, and it was soon under-stood that no thought of hostilities existed in the minds of either tribe.

A peaceful night came slowly down over the immense prairie.

After the customary exchange of gifts, there were friendly feasts in both camps. The *bois brûlés* had been far from any fort or trading post for a long time, and their whiskey keg was almost empty. This greatly displeased the French Crees, for they were notorious drunkards. There remained enough liquor, however, for several men of both tribes to get thoroughly crazy. They made the peaceful night intolerable with their singing and bellowing, but as the dawn approached all disturbances began to cease. By early morning both camps were wrapped in deep slumber.

Yesa, however, could not sleep. He lay upon his couch in the darkness and stared up through the smoke hole into the sky. He was thinking about Tatanka. He had sworn to avenge his death, and yet he had never been in battle. It was almost his seventeenth summer and still he had not killed a single Gros Ventre or white man. How could he become a great and famous warrior among his people if he did not soon go on the warpath?

Yesa closed his eyes and thought about his father and brothers who had been murdered by the soldiers. He thought about the white men and women he had watched madly dancing at the trading post of Fort Ellis. And he tried to imagine what it would be like to kill one of them.

He knew almost nothing about the Long Knives, as his people called the white men. He had been very young when he lived among the settlers in Minnesota, before the uprising had caused his tribe to escape into their long and sorrowful exile. And he had already been adopted into the family of Uncheedah and his uncle Mysterious Medicine when his father had been betrayed and murdered at Mankato.

Among Indian people it was a great deed to avenge the death of a relative or of a dear friend, and Mysterious Medicine had accordingly spared no efforts to instill into Yesa's mind the obligation to avenge the death of his father and his older brothers. Yesa accepted this responsibility and had always looked forward to the day when he would meet the Long Knives in battle.

And yet he could not hate them. In some ways he distrusted them greatly, but in another he'd heard such remarkable things about them, he regarded them as a race whose power bordered upon the supernatural!

For a long while Yesa lay awake, peering up at the sky and thinking about the Long Knives. Then he glanced across the dark lodge and, hearing a gentle rustle, whispered, "Uncheedah . . . are you asleep?"

"Now I am not asleep—you crazy boy. What is the matter?" she said.

"Nothing," he whispered. But then he added, "Uncheedah, tell me about the Long Knives. I want to know more about the Long Knives."

"Yes . . . yes . . . in the morning I will tell you about anything you want to know, but now it is time to sleep. If you continue to talk you will surely awaken your uncle and he will be very angry and blame me for fussing over you. So go to sleep!"

"Oh," muttered Yesa, "nothing besides an enemy attack could awaken Mysterious Medicine. He can sleep through a victory dance!"

"Do not make fun of your uncle," Uncheedah said.

"I promise that I will not make fun of him if you will tell me about the Long Knives, Grandmother. Then I promise you, I will go to sleep and not bother you again tonight!"

"Ai . . ." Uncheedah moaned, raising herself onto her elbows and shaking her head. "Then tell me, what must you know about the Long Knives that is so important that your grandmother cannot sleep?"

"Tell me about the fire-boat! Tell me about the fire-boat that you saw, Uncheedah."

For a moment there was silence and then Grandmother said, "It is true, my son, the Long Knives have made a fire-boat-walks-on-mountains! It is a miracle that they have created, for it is said that this monster flies from mountain to mountain when it gets excited. And it must surely contain within its body the great Thunderbird, for as the fire-boat-walks-on-mountains speeds along it makes the great roar of thunder! Several of our warriors have observed it closely. And from them I learned that this monster of the Long Knives cannot walk except upon the iron track that is laid down on the ground for it to crawl upon. Therefore, it cannot chase the warriors into rough country."

Yesa was greatly relieved to hear that at least the fire-boat-walks-on-mountains could not chase a warrior. So perhaps the magic of the Long Knives was not so great that an Indian might be unable to avenge the death of a father! It was said that the white men made houses over the Missouri and Mississippi rivers so they could cross over them without going into the water! And more than that, Yesa had also heard they made immense houses of stone and brick, piled on top of one another until they were as high as mountains!

"Uncheedah . . ." he whispered.

"Ai . . . not again! What must you know now?" his grand-mother muttered.

"The Long Knives must be a very heartless nation, for they have made slaves of some of their people."

"That is true," Uncheedah said sadly, "they painted some of their servants black a very long time ago, so they could separate them from the rest of the people. Now these slaves have children born to them of the same color! That is another bad magic of the Long Knives. The greatest object of their lives seems to be the collecting of many, many things. They are always collecting things. For thirty summers they tried to get us to sell them our land in Minnesota. And finally when the uprising took place, they took everything from us without giving us anything in return and forced us to run away. That is how the Long Knives are. No one understands such a crazy nation of people! They count everything. They have divided the day into parts and each day has a name. They measure and count everything. Not one of them would let so much as a turnip go uncounted in his field! And I understand that some of them make a great feast and invite many people, but when the dinner is over the guests are required to pay for what they have eaten before they leave the house! I myself saw at White Cliff a man who kept a brass drum and a bell to call people to his table, but when he got them in he would make them pay for the food! They are crazy, these Long Knives.

Some of them are *black robes.* They came to visit with us in Minnesota before our exile began. They observed every seventh day as a holy day. And on that particular day they met in a house built just for that purpose—to sing and pray and speak of their Great Mystery. I was never in one of those houses, but I understand that they had a very large book from which they read. They sang of peace and they prayed for tranquillity, but when the sacred day was over they did not keep the peace and they would not allow Indians tranquillity. They are a strange people who have no spirit. They fight among themselves and they fight against Indians. They do all this fighting not for honor but simply to gain possession of more things, of more land. . . . Always, always, they want more and more things. It is a madness of theirs, this hunger to possess everything they see!"

"But why—" Yesa began, but his grandmother interrupted him sternly.

"Enough! Go to sleep! . . . Go to sleep or you will wake up so tired you will turn into an old man and never see a Long Knife and never go on the warpath. Go to sleep!"

Yesa closed his eyes.

Silence fell upon the lodge and now nothing moved but the necklace of stars that circled the vast black night.

Yesa had already begun to invoke the blessing of the Great Mystery. Scarcely a day passed that he did not offer up some of

the game he shot when he went hunting. He had willingly sac-
rificed his favorite possessions ever since the day Uncheedah had
helped him make his first offering. His youthful ways were fast
departing, and now a sober dignity and composure were trans-
forming Yesa into an adult. He gave all his thoughts to the Great
Mystery, for he alone could give a young man the vision that
would provide his whole life with meaning. He gave no thought
to the pretty girls of his camp, for he had a dream of someday,
when he had made his reputation and won the eagle feathers of
a great man, courting his dear cousin Oesedah!

A cool breeze swept through the lodge, and Yesa smiled and
rolled over. Before him drifted the face of little Oesedah, smiling
shyly and slowly nodding her head. Her long black hair twisted
gently into the air as two thousand ponies fell asleep in the
moonlit meadow of her forehead. The flute of love made its
music, and the river left its banks and danced with the Moon.

# THE DEAD

Now it was the fall, and the tribe had drifted toward the southern part of Manitoba. It was a fine September morning as Yesa got up and discovered an unusual air of excitement in the camp. Uncheedah came running into the lodge and embraced him.

"It is a miracle!" she stammered. "Many Lightnings . . . your father, Many Lightnings! He has come, Yesa! It is true! The father we thought dead at the hands of the white men, he has come back to life!"

It was a day of many miracles on the vast plains of Manitoba. Many Lightnings had come back from the dead. Dressed in curious black clothes, his elegant black hair hacked off at the ears and plastered down upon his head, this white man with an Indian's face said that he was Yesa's father, come home after ten long winters.

But how could this be? How could this stranger be Yesa's father? The man's stern face was unfamiliar. His eyes were filled with something Yesa had never before seen in the eyes of an Indian. And though he spoke the language of the tribe without difficulty, he said his name was no longer Many Lightnings. He said he had been transformed by the white holy men, and his new name was *Jacob East.*

Yesa repeated the name to himself again and again, trying to understand what it meant. He stared at the man who was his father and blinked his eyes. Everyone stood in a silent circle, gazing in bewilderment at this Indian wearing a black, baggy suit, stiff white shirt, and shiny black shoes. He looked so much like a stuffed doll that a little boy burst out laughing at the strange sight, but his mother quickly silenced him.

Who could believe such a thing? How was it possible for an Indian to be so utterly transformed by the white men? Surely it was their magic that had done this terrible thing to Many Lightnings!

Uncheedah peered at her firstborn son and groaned. She gasped when she saw how his beautiful black hair was chopped off. And when he embraced her she knew that his heart was dead, for the touch of his hand was cold and alien.

Mysterious Medicine let out a wild whoop of joy when he saw his brother. He was jubilant that he had survived the captivity of the white soldiers and had not been executed with the other Indian prisoners. But Many Lightnings did not greet his beloved brother with affection. He made a curious gesture, taking Mysterious Medicine's hand and wagging it to and fro as if he wished to shake it off. The expression on Mysterious Medicine's happy face changed abruptly, for this man who looked so much like his brother was no longer the same person. He was utterly different, a stranger to his own people.

No one spoke. The people stared awkwardly at one another. A great sadness flowed slowly into Uncheedah's eyes and tears began to fall. But Jacob East did not notice the bewilderment and sorrow of his family. He did not seem to see anybody as he carefully searched the crowd. Then abruptly he smiled when he saw his son standing among the people.

"You are Hakadah!" he exclaimed, taking Yesa by the shoulders and laughing happily as he peered at him. He then asked after Chatanna and when he was told that he had been given away, he nodded solemnly for only a moment and returned his attention to Yesa.

Yesa did not know what to say or what to do. He could not look this stranger in the face. And yet he tried to greet him warmly. He tried to treat him with respect and honor, for Jacob East was his father, and during every day of his life Yesa had been taught to respect his parents and to listen silently to their instructions and their wishes.

"It is for you that I have returned," Jacob East told his son. "It is only for you that I have come back, for I have found something wonderful and new in the ten years that I have been gone. Now it is my duty to impart all these wonders unto you, my son."

Uncheedah turned her back. She would not look at or speak to Many Lightnings. It then became the job of Mysterious Medicine to call upon young Oesedah to prepare a meal for the guest and to welcome him properly.

"It would have been better," Uncheedah moaned, "if he had stayed dead. Once he was a great warrior among our people. Now he is nothing. He is not a white man and he is not an Indian. And I am ashamed to be his mother."

Mysterious Medicine tried to comfort his mother, but she would not remain in the lodge. She went out into the evening and walked deep into the desolation of the prairie, where she wept and prayed, mourning the second death of her firstborn son.

In the night and in the days that followed, Jacob East spoke to no one but Yesa. He avoided the company of the other people of his tribe and devoted all his time to long and eloquent conversations with Yesa.

It was only because this stranger was his honored father that Yesa lent his attention to the long speeches he made each day and each night. It was for this reason alone that Yesa listened to him talk about the vastness and wonders of the white man's world. Yesa could not doubt his own father, so mysteriously returned from the spirit land, yet as he listened to the tales of the ways of the white man, there was a voice within him loudly saying: "No! It is a false life! I would not live such a life!"

He asked few questions as his father preached to him, although many arose in his perplexed thoughts. Yesa tried to fit these strange thoughts into the teachings he had been given since the day of his birth. But nothing seemed to fit! He struggled to retain the teachings of his grandmother and Mysterious Medicine at the same time he attempted to respect the wisdom of his father's words. He truly wanted to please his father, but everything within him cried out against what his father said. Only gradually did the purpose of his father's sermons occur to Yesa.

"My son, I have come to take you with me to the glorious new life I have found!"

Yesa pulled back and groaned with dismay. He wanted to run away from his father. He wanted to strike him with all his might and run away in shame. "It is false and wrong!" he whimpered as he turned to his uncle in the hope that he would cry out against such treachery. But Mysterious Medicine bowed his head sadly. "Yesa," he murmured, "this man is your father and you must honor him and obey him. That is the way of our people."

"But it is not the way of our people to love the white man and to wish to live in his world!" Yesa exclaimed.

"Silence!" Mysterious Medicine ordered. "Do not speak to your father with such anger or you will make me ashamed of you, Yesa." And then his uncle sighed and glanced with hostility at the man now called Jacob East. "He is your son," he said sullenly, "but for ten winters I have been his father and Uncheedah has been his mother. We taught him the ways of our ancestors so you might be proud of him. And we showed him the good life of our people. Now he is a man. He is a young warrior who dreamed of avenging his father's murder. And now you ask him to love the very soldiers who killed his brothers and captured you. You ask him to love the white men who took you away from him for ten winters! It is not easy, my brother . . . for Uncheedah and for Mysterious Medicine . . . it is not easy. But for this young man it is even harder. So I ask you, if you must take him away from us now, be kind and be gentle to him, for it might drive him mad to go back with you into the world of the dead from which you have escaped!''

With this Mysterious Medicine left the lodge and Yesa found himself alone with his father. He was in a panic to escape, but he knew he could not do so. As much as Mysterious Medicine and Uncheedah and all the holy people loathed the words Jacob East was telling his son, they would not interfere. And as much as Yesa feared this stern man with cold eyes and strong voice, he could not run away from him because he was his father. This was the custom of the people and there was only dishonor to he who broke that tradition.

"Our life here in the plains," said his father, "I admit to you is the best life. But there is a race that has learned things so wonderful that I could not at first believe they existed. They know how to weigh and how to measure everything—time and labor and vegetables and stones. They have knowledge that allows them to accumulate and preserve wealth for future generations. You yourself use some of the wonderful inventions of the white man: his guns and gunpowder, his knives and hatchets, garments of every description, and thousands upon thousands of other things that are both useful and marvelous! But, above all, they have a Great Teacher whom they call Jesus and He instructed them to pass on His wisdom to all the primitive races. It is true! All that I have told you is true, my son. These white men are more numerous than the clouds in the sky. And they are powerful. Already they have traveled across the entire land—to places we have never dreamed about—across oceans and rivers; and they have taken the teachings of Jesus with them to all the people of the far-flung lands. And now our race must also bow to the lessons and the laws of the white man. The sooner we accept their way of life and follow their teachings the better it will be for all of us. For ten years I have thought about this, my son, and such are my conclusions!"

Yesa could not speak. He stared at his father and tried to think of something to say. He began to tremble, and he felt sick and faint. He wanted to shout. He wanted to open his throat and bellow with rage and sorrow and fear. But he could not speak.

Then slowly, for the first time in many winters, the young warrior bowed his head and tears flowed down his cheeks.

The line between Canada and the United States was closely watched by Indians, for these were the days of great wars between the tribes and the soldiers. Therefore Jacob East told his son that it was best for them to make a dash for Devil's Lake, in North Dakota, where it was possible to get assistance from the white men there.

"I know a powerful man named Major Forbes who is in command of the military post and the agency at Devil's Lake. He will help us reach safety," Jacob East said.

Yesa could not understand what his father was saying. "Safety?" he asked, shaking his head with bewilderment. "Safety among the soldiers who have chased us for ten years?"

"There are hostile savages everywhere!" his father explained. "If they discover our attempt to escape they will kill us! Do you understand?"

Yesa nodded with confusion, but he was afraid to ask any further questions, for each answer his father gave made him only more confused.

"These Indians will stop at nothing. I myself was betrayed by a half-breed and sent to prison. But the heathen did not realize what a blessing it was to be captured, for it was in the prison that I learned the ways of the white man and discovered the teachings of Jesus! Do you see? There was a reason that I was captured!"

Then Jacob East slipped out of the lodge and went in search of the half-breed who had helped him find the whereabouts of Yesa's people. In the ten years since Jacob East was Many Lightnings, the great warrior, he had forgotten the land and could no longer find his way over the great prairie without the assistance of a guide.

The half-breed, his father told Yesa, would lead them to Devil's Lake. "But he is an unscrupulous man who would betray us for a kettle of whiskey or a pony. So we must pray before we leave camp and ask Jesus to protect us from treachery!"

Yesa whimpered as his father pulled him to his knees and held him tightly with one arm, while with the other he took a small black book from his pocket and began to whisper.

Yesa could not understand the words. He could not understand how it was possible for a man to speak aloud to the Great Mystery. And he was ashamed to be kneeling on the ground while his father madly mumbled these strange words.

"Come now, my son, before anybody misses us!" Jacob East whispered urgently as he pulled Yesa to his feet and urged him to step outside the lodge where the half-breed was waiting with horses and supplies for their journey.

"But Uncheedah . . ." Yesa stammered.

"There is no time . . . there is no time for goodbyes! We must leave at once or we will be in grave danger!"

"In danger from my grandmother?" Yesa whispered. "In danger from my own people? What are you saying?"

"There is no time! Listen to me, for I am your father, and I am telling you that there is no time for goodbyes! We must hurry before it gets light!''

Helplessly, Yesa mounted his pony. He searched the dark camp for Mysterious Medicine, he whispered Oesedah's name, and he called out to Uncheedah. He felt that he could not bear leaving without saying farewell to those he loved. But the halfbreed suddenly whipped their horses, and they rushed into the night.

Yesa kept looking back as his horse swiftly carried him into the utter blackness of the prairie. The campfires vanished. The lodges of his people were swallowed by the darkness. Nothing remained except his bursting heart and a blizzard of stars that fluttered all around him.

"Be on your guard!" Jacob East muttered as they galloped through the night. "There are Indians everywhere!"

Yesa shouted. "No! No! No! I will not go!" But the halfbreed whipped Yesa's pony and with a burst of energy the animal dashed headlong toward the edge of the world where dawn was slowly making its crimson dance.

"No! No! No!" Yesa shouted again and again.

But nothing could save him now.

"The Lord . . . is my shepherd . . ." Jacob East mumbled urgently as he peered into the gray landscape, watching anxiously for Indians, ". . . I shall not want. He maketh me . . . to lie down in green pastures . . ."

"No! No!" Yesa wailed as he looked back toward the distant camp of his people. Now nothing remained. The sweet grass. The sound of the loon. The songs of morning. Nothing remained.

". . . He leadeth me beside the still waters . . . He restoreth my soul . . ." Jacob East whispered incessantly as they hurried over the bleak plains toward Devil's Lake.

Yesa wept bitterly. He opened his heart and cried great tears of lamentation. He wept for the good days and the buffalo and the little mice who were lost among the stars and could not find their way home again.

". . . He leadeth me in the paths of righteousness . . . for His name's sake . . ."

He wept for Oesedah who would never be his wife. And he ached for Uncheedah and for the willows and the river and the ancient voice of his people that sang through his veins and called out to him.

". . . Yea, though I walk through the valley of the shadow of death . . ."

And then Yesa became silent and closed an immense sorrow within himself. "Ai . . ." he whispered in despair as he slowly turned away in the darkness, leaving a trail of smoke and ashes behind him.

# WHITE MAN

**H**e stood, dumbfounded, beside a rude log cabin, overlooking the leafy basin of the Big Sioux River. Each day since he had left Canada had been a day of bewilderment.

Yesa had stumbled wide-eyed behind his father as they journeyed into this new world. At the place called Jamestown a terrifying peal of thunder burst from a spotless blue sky and ran along the ground like a deluge. The ponies stampeded and Yesa was not far behind them, when a monster with one fiery eye poked its roaring head around the corner of a hill.

Jamestown was the terminal point of the Northern Pacific railroad, and Jacob East explained to his fearful son that this monster, this fire-boat-walks-on-mountains, was called a "train." He added that it was a means of getting from one place to another and that they would travel in it to Devil's Lake.

With the greatest of misgivings Yesa reached toward the men riding inside the monster and allowed them to pull him in after them.

"It is going to be all right," his father kept whispering to him. "Everything is going to be fine."

Inside the train there were many white men sitting on peculiar objects that held them high above the floor. Jacob East gestured for his son to be seated, and Yesa lowered himself into the awkward position in which the other men were sitting.

No sooner had he taken his position than he heard the same roar of thunder that had frightened the ponies when the fire-boat first came chugging around the hill. Yesa bolted for the open air, but before he could leap to safety his father and several white men grabbed hold of him. Yesa shouted wildly and tried to free himself as he saw the ground begin to move. It moved faster and faster until it vanished into a dreadful blur. The monster shook and panted and twisted under his feet, swaying so violently that he had to grasp its exposed metal ribs to remain standing.

"Come, sit down," his father said gently.

Fearfully he took his place in the careening fire-boat next to Jacob East, squatting uncomfortably on one of the smooth green objects on which all the white people were sitting. Hesitantly he glanced through the many eyes of the beast that looked out upon the fleeting world. The sight of the grass and trees flying past him was more than he could bear, and before long he began to feel dizzy. When his father opened a hole in one of the monster's eyes, Yesa lunged for the opening and hung out into the rushing wind as he vomited and shouted and begged to be sent back to his people.

Now he stood beside the log cabin of his father and gazed over the rolling prairie land that stretched toward the horizon from the banks of the Big Sioux River. The vastness of the new land frightened Yesa. The sky threatened him with its emptiness. There was nothing in this strange region that did not terrify him.

Jacob East's farm lay along the north bank of the river. The nearest neighbor lived very far away. There were no people and there was no grass. In every direction were rigid rows of wheat and corn and potatoes. There was no place in this land where the people had not left the scars of their shovels and plows. There was no place left for the elk or the buffalo. Occasionally a rabbit made its terrified way among the furrows, trying to escape into the wilderness. But there was nowhere to run. In every direction the earth was ravaged and torn and cut into pieces. Where the fires had burned and the singing voices had echoed in the tall grass, there was now a gray, silent land. All the birds had lost their way and all the tipis were gone.

There was nothing to see in any direction except two imposing and fantastic structures that rose in the distance above the corn-fields. The mission church and the schoolhouse, the only build-ings within many miles, stood proudly where the Big Sioux River doubled back upon itself in a swirling loop.

Every morning it was Yesa's duty to bring his father's small herd of ponies into the log corral. But this morning, he lingered and gazed out toward the northern horizon where his people still lived contented and free. Turning to look at the ponies, he noticed they too were unwilling to be driven into the corral. Like Yesa, they loved their freedom and would not easily come in from grazing.

Jacob East, in his baggy black pants and white shirt, also stood beside the cabin, the first house he had ever built. He stood there, his face resolute, watching his son.

He had lived all his life in a buffalo-skin lodge, until the day he had been made prisoner of the white man. It was, he ex-plained to Yesa, because of his conversion to Christianity in a military prison that he had decided to abandon his tribe and take up a homestead. "I will never again have anything to do with an Indian uprising! Never again! For the rest of my days I am going to work with my hands and praise Jesus Christ, my Savior!"

These were Jacob East's firm convictions, and he believed in them so strongly that he was able to persuade a few Indian families to join him. They had worked with him to form a little colony at Flandreau, on the banks of the Big Sioux River. And it was here that Jacob East wanted his son to spend the rest of his life.

"Now," his father said, walking over to Yesa, "it is time for you to go to the school. You must learn the English language and you must learn something about books. That is the right and just way for Indians if we are to survive!"

"And, father," Yesa asked finally, with much embarrassment, "what am I to do at the school?"

"You will be taught the way the white man speaks, and you will learn how to count your money and how to tell the price of your horses and of your corn and wheat. The teacher will teach you the marks by which words are made in books. All these things you must learn quickly and well."

Yesa stood quietly, staring at his father without knowing what to say. Finally Jacob East pointed sternly into the distance where strange buildings jutted into the air.

"It is time now. You will go to the mission school today," he said.

"Ai . . ." Yesa mumbled sadly as he turned to fetch his pony.

Soon he was on his way to the school although he had absolutely no idea what he had to do there. He dutifully galloped along the dirt road trying to understand his father's wishes.

"But why should there be marks in a book when people can hear and talk?" he said aloud as he pulled on the lariat and brought his pony to a stop.

Many questions nagged him as his horse grazed in the early sunshine. Yesa leaned back in the warmth and closed his eyes.

Suddenly he was startled by yells. He turned around and pulled his pony's head up just as two Indian boys stopped their panting horses at his side. They stared at Yesa for a long time, while he looked back cautiously.

"Where are you going? Are you going to our school?" one of the boys asked at last.

Yesa replied timidly. "My father told me to go to a place where the white man's ways are taught, and to learn the sign language of books."

"That's good! We are going there too! Come on, we are having a race to the school. Will you race with us?"

No sooner had the boys spoken than they dashed off at full speed. Yesa laughed when he saw the young strangers riding as erect as soldiers. That is because they have been taught to be white men, he thought with a grin. I must remind them how an Indian rides his horse!

He allowed his pony a free start and leaned forward until the great animal beneath him drew deep breaths, then he slid back and laid his head against his pony's shoulder, at the same time raising his quirt. At once the animal lunged forward at great speed. Yesa yelled joyously as he overtook the young men, and pulled up when he reached the crossing to wait for them.

When they stopped beside Yesa they looked at him in earnest respect and amazement, carefully surveying him and his pony from head to hoof as if they had never seen anyone ride so fast before.

"You have a fast pony. Where did you get him?" one of the boys asked.

"I brought him with me from Canada. I am the son of Many Lightnings, who has brought me here to live with him."

"You are lucky to have such a fast horse!" the other boy exclaimed with admiration.

Yesa was very proud. "My uncle, Mysterious Medicine, always used to ride him in Canada to chase buffalo. And he has also ridden him in many battles!"

"Well," the first boy said with a frown, "there are no more

battles and there are no more buffalo, so your pony will have to pull the plow like all the rest."

By this time they had reached the riverbank where the mission school stood. There were thirty or forty Indian children standing around the squat little building, curiously watching the newcomer as he rode up the steep bank.

An immense embarrassment suddenly seized Yesa. For the first time in his life he felt like an object of curiosity, and it was a terrible sensation. But at the very same time he was being stared at, he was also staring back at the strange appearance of the students. They were all wearing odd imitations of white man's clothing. The students were wearing pantaloons that were either too long or too short and coats that only met halfway around their bodies and were held together with strings. Some of their hats did not have brims and others were without crowns. The boys' hair was chopped off so that it bristled in every direction like porcupine quills.

As Yesa stood and looked at this motley gathering, he thought that he had never seen Indians look more foolish. If he had to look like these fellows in order to obtain something of the white man's learnings, then it was surely time for him to rebel!

While the other boys played ball, Yesa tied his pony to a tree and walked self-consciously to the steps of the schoolhouse. He stood there as silent and motionless as if he were a tree. He did not know whether to jump on his pony and run away or to obey his father and remain at the school. Before he could decide, a man came out of the building and rang a bell. All of the young men and women quickly filed into the school, but Yesa waited outside for a long time before entering. Finally, summoning up his courage, he cautiously slid inside the one-room building and took the seat nearest the door. He felt utterly out of place, and desperately fought back the immense sadness in his chest born of his wish to be back among his own people in Canada.

When the teacher spoke, Yesa did not have the slightest idea what he was saying, so he remained silent for fear of giving offense. Finally the teacher asked very falteringly in Yesa's language: "What is your name?"

Clearly this white man had not been among Indians very long, or he would not have asked such a personal question. Yesa was dumbfounded by the teacher's bad manners. But he asked the question again and again, until finally he frowned down at Yesa and returned to his seat on the platform.

The teacher then said some words to the class that Yesa again could not understand. The other pupils immediately opened the books on their desks and began to talk in a strange language. After this the teacher got up and made some signs on a black wall and pointed to these marks as if the students were supposed to say something about them. To Yesa these scratches did not begin to compare in interest to the tracks of birds. In fact he had seen nothing so far that proved to him that the white man's ways were of any value!

Meanwhile the students grew bolder and began to whisper about the "new boy" and his strange appearance. Yesa tried to ignore the grins of the young men as they stared at him with disapproval. Finally one of the older boys muttered the Indian word for "baby," and Yesa was completely mortified. He silently got up and walked to the door. He did not dare say anything as he left the room, though he was angry enough to shout at all of them. The boys watched him from the window as Yesa led his pony to the river to drink and then jumped on the animal's back to start for home. As he galloped over the hill, he could hear the children cheering: "Hooo-ooo! There goes the long-haired Indian!"

Yesa was afraid to return to the cabin. He spent the whole long day dreaming sadly on the riverbank. It was already growing dark when he at last arrived at his father's cabin.

"What is the matter with you?" Jacob East asked with a look of dissatisfaction on his proud face.

Yesa could not speak. His melancholy was so great that he feared he would shame himself before his father by weeping if he tried to explain.

"Answer me!" the old man shouted angrily. "When a son is asked a question he is supposed to answer!"

Yesa swallowed hard and stared at the floor while his father stood impatiently awaiting his response. "I am not . . ." he stammered, "I am not . . . one of them."

Jacob East frowned. "What do you mean?" he said more gently. "What do you mean . . . you are not one of them?"

Yesa clenched his fists as he desperately tried to find words. "They . . . they are no longer . . . they are not like our people anymore. They . . ."

"What do you mean? What is the matter with you, my son?"

Then Yesa glanced uncertainly at his father and blurted out: "Why do you always say 'my son'? Why do you never call me by my name? What is happening here and why do all those children behave as if they were no longer Indians?"

Jacob East pounded violently on the table just once. "Silence!" he exclaimed. For a moment he looked as if he might strike his son, but as abruptly as the rage had overtaken him it seemed to disappear. He wearily lowered himself into a wooden chair and nodded his head in silence. For a very long time he did not speak. Then at last he murmured: "You must learn to get along with the other pupils. That is your duty. You must find your way in this new world or you will not survive. And one day soon, when you learn to pray, then you will receive the help of Jesus Christ in these times of trouble."

"Ai . . ." Yesa mumbled defiantly, the tears coming into his eyes. "But could the Great Mystery make such a mistake as this? Is it not against our faith to change the customs that we have practiced for many ages?"

Jacob East listened in silence, deeply saddened by his son's many tears. But then he interrupted with a resolute speech. "I am one Indian who will sacrifice everything—all the ages of custom and all the generations of living like savages—to win the wisdom of the white man! We have entered upon this life, and there is no turning back."

Yesa's eyes were fixed upon the burning logs in the huge fireplace in the corner of the cabin. He was watching the flames flickering and jumping into the chimney, reaching into the air for their freedom.

"You must give me your word," his father said at last, "to return to the school and to make me proud of you."

Yesa did not want to go back to the school again. He did not want to live in the white man's world. But he could not defy his father. And so the next morning he sat grimly in the chair by the table while Jacob East used a large hunting knife to hack off his marvelous long hair. The locks fell one by one to the floor like so many irretrievable memories. Yesa became sick and dizzy as he felt his father tug at his hair. As he heard the knife cut into his memory and slice away the ages and the generations of his people, making an everlasting scar in his mind. He stared down at the floor where the black silk tumbled slowly, twisting in the breeze, fluttering into the dusty corners of the cabin where the field mice scampered after it, pulling it into their forlorn little dens where they wove the nests of their eternal exile.

# NEW WORLD

It was in the fall of 1874 that Yesa left his father's cabin in Flandreau and started out for the mission school of Dr. Alfred L. Riggs in Nebraska. The young man had obeyed his father's wishes and had become a good student. He quickly learned to read, write, and speak the English language better than any of the other students of the little Indian community of Flandreau. His achievements in school were so excellent that the teacher had urged Jacob East to send his son to Nebraska, where Dr. Riggs had recently established a renowned mission school for the training of the best-educated Indians of the day.

The thought of traveling deeper and deeper into the world of the white man both intrigued and frightened Yesa. And yet, as his father had told him, there was no turning back.

On the day of his departure from his father's cabin, Yesa sat silently thinking many solemn thoughts. His own people were far behind him—in the windy, open plains of the northwest where there were no farms or schools or books. Sitting Bull and Crazy Horse—the greatest warriors of his people—were still fighting for freedom, battling soldiers and immigrants who wished to take away the ancient lands. But the days of the old life were running out. Yesa knew that the good days were ending. From his vantage at the very brink of the oncoming tide of white civilization along the banks of the Big Sioux River, he could see the hopelessness of the fight that brave warriors were still fighting in the far West. Each day more whites swarmed across the land. Each night their fires became more numerous and the sound of their voices overwhelmed the whisper of the Great Mystery. General Custer had just been placed in military command of the Dakota Territory, and the most terrible of all their days were yet to come for Yesa's people.

Within his mind there were now two languages speaking out against each other. There were so many new ideas that they made him confused and frightened. But in his heart there was still only one voice. Troubled and saddened by his departure, he went to the place where all his people had gone for generations when they sought peace and understanding—into the deep woods.

Yesa wanted a wiser word that came from something stronger and bigger than the minds of men. He needed something that confirmed the greatest convictions of his heart. And so he did what he had been taught to do; he sought the Great Mystery in silence, in the deep forest.

As he walked slowly among the green shadows of the singular stand of trees that remained in the vast, nude farmlands, he trembled in fear that the Great Mystery might no longer recognize him. His beautiful hair was gone. His buckskin leggings, his blanket, his bear's claw necklace—all traces of his nobility—had been taken away from him. He knew nothing of the white man's religion despite Jacob East's prayers and insistent lectures, and yet he was afraid that he had traveled too far from the land where the Great Mystery filled the world with wonderment. He was frightened to think that he might no longer be able to find his way back into the sky where the Great Mystery spoke in the wind.

But in the silence of the woods there came a miracle into Yesa's ears. There came a singing. The few remaining animals peered cautiously out at him until they recognized his face. And then they cried out to him, mourning for the many trees that had been cut and burned. They lamented the loss of each blade of grass that had been trampled and buried by the plows. They spoke to Yesa as they had spoken to him since his childhood, showing him the way among the trees lest he get lost in the shadows of men's eyes.

When Yesa came out of the little woods his heart was strong. He was ready to follow his new trail to its end. He knew that just as a little brook leads to larger and larger streams until it becomes a restless, surging river, so must he explore the great things ahead of him. The immensity of his destiny made him shiver to think of it. But once again he recalled the teachings of his people, and he was more determined than ever to carry their tradition of bravery and spirited adventure. If only he could achieve acceptance in the white world, then perhaps he could one day return and help glorify and nourish the sacred tree of his people. He stood among the green shadows of that little forest on the banks of the Big Sioux River and resolved to move forward, though he could hardly imagine what he would encounter along the way.

Yesa embraced Jacob East. His father had arranged his son's passage to Nebraska with a neighbor who was en route to that region. There were only a few small houses in the vicinity, and the whole countryside seemed desolate and lonely when they silently embarked in a rude, homemade prairie schooner on that bright September morning.

"Remember, my son," Jacob East called out dolefully, "it is as if I am sending you on your first warpath. I expect you to be victorious!"

Yesa waved at the diminishing figure standing against the wide blue morning sky. Then he turned away quickly as an enormous fear and loneliness filled him.

Now he was alone. He still had his Hudson Bay flintlock gun, which he had brought down from Canada. And he had an extra shirt. But that was all he owned besides the baggy clothes he wore. He was eighteen years old and there was no one left to befriend him now. Everything he trusted and loved vanished into the distance. Before him was an unspeakable and fearsome future. He drew a deep breath and set his eyes upon the dream of the unknown, as the covered wagon lurched and rolled into a strange new world.

The bell of the old chapel at Santee summoned the pupils to class. The principal, Dr. Alfred L. Riggs, read aloud from a large black book. He was a remarkable-looking person, with a large hairless head, a narrow fringe that bristled around his ears, and a voluminous white bush that covered his mouth and hung from his chin. He was as pale as the belly of a snake and his eyes were as green as two river stones, and yet he spoke the Indian language as clearly and elegantly as a chief. And although he conducted the prayer in Yesa's own language, the names and the words were strange and unintelligible. He understood that the principal was praying to the Great Mystery, but he was appalled that Dr. Riggs asked the Great Mystery to stay with the pupils during their day's work. It seemed far too much to ask! All his life Yesa had been instructed that the power of life could only be addressed in the seclusion of nature. But here for the first time he heard people asking small favors of the Great Mystery in a chapel filled with many people.

After the prayer the students were sent to separate rooms to study under different teachers. Yesa was left in the chapel with another man. He was a Mandan Indian who had just arrived from Fort Berthold. Yesa was appalled when he learned the fellow's tribe, for the Mandan were ancient enemies of his people. It was unthinkable to sit in the same room with such a person! Only a few years earlier Mysterious Medicine had been on the warpath against this enemy tribe and had brought home two Mandan scalps. Yesa scowled at the young man and turned his back on him.

They sat together in the chapel for a very long time. Neither of them spoke. Gradually their anxiety as new students overcame their animosity. Yesa glanced uncertainly at the Mandan. He still had beautiful long hair arranged in two braids, and in spite of his forlorn face he was a noble-looking fellow. To Yesa, he appeared to be at a very great advantage in comparison to the other students, whose hair was chopped shorter than Yesa's pathetic locks and whose clothes had none of the elegance of the Indian wardrobe.

The two young men did not speak, but they looked with a sense of comradery at each other.

Soon Dr. Riggs called to Yesa and took him into a little office, where he politely explained the rules of the school. He also described the mission school's facilities. There was a chapel that was used as a church every Sunday. There was the Dakota Home, the girls' dormitory, and for the boys there was a long loghouse located under a grove of large cottonwood trees.

"It is not necessary for you to start studying on your first day," Dr. Riggs said with a smile, putting his fingers into the bush that hung from his chin as if he were hunting for something hidden away inside the tangle of hairs. "You may fill up this big bag with fresh straw from the pile you will find behind the barn. Then carry it over to the boys' loghouse, where you have been provided a bunk to sleep in. Do you understand?"

Yesa nodded silently and followed the instructions carefully. When he arrived at the dormitory Dr. Riggs was there to greet him and to give him two sheets and a blanket. Then, while the doctor looked on with interest, Yesa made his first white man's bed, again carefully following Dr. Riggs's instructions.

"You must make your bed every morning just as I have shown you. Is that clear? And you must wash yourself. There is a tin basin on the bench just outside the dormitory. And there are two big water barrels. Do you know how to wash yourself?"

Yesa nodded silently.

Then Dr. Riggs smiled again and asked, "What does your father call you?"

The question was so politely asked that Yesa could not avoid answering. "Yesa," he murmured with embarrassment.

Again Dr. Riggs smiled, and after a moment's thought he asked, "And what is your father called?"

"Many Lightnings."

"But I understood that your father is a Christian gentleman. Doesn't he have a Christian's name, my son?"

For a moment Yesa was reluctant to pronounce the peculiar name his father had been given by the church. "Jacob . . . Jacob East," he murmured.

"Ah yes, now that is a fine name, isn't it? And what do you think we should call you?" Dr. Riggs asked with a smile.

Yesa did not wish to give up his name. It was a name that had been given to him by the holy men of his tribe. It was an honorable name, which celebrated his victory in the game of lacrosse. He did not wish to give his name away.

Dr. Riggs continued to smile at Yesa as he awaited his answer. When the boy didn't speak the old man cleared his throat and shrewdly asked, "And what is it about your good father that makes you most proud? Perhaps that is an easier question to answer."

At once Yesa said, "He was one of the great warriors of my people before he was captured and taken from us!"

"Ah," murmured Dr. Riggs, "then I think I have a good name for you. Have you ever heard of a very famous man whose name was Alexander the Great?"

Yesa shook his head and confessed that he had not.

"Well, my boy, he was a very important warrior—perhaps the most important warrior who ever lived. So what would you think of having his name?"

Yesa did not respond. He did not wish to give away his name and accept the name of some white man, but he did not dare defy Dr. Riggs.

"Then it is settled," the doctor said with a friendly laugh. "You will be known as Alexander East! What a very distinguished name that is for you!"

Yesa nodded and looked down at the floor, feeling dreadfully injured at having suddenly been deprived of the name he had worked so hard to win.

"That will be all, Alexander," Dr. Riggs said. "You may go outside now and explore the grounds until lunchtime."

Yesa bowed awkwardly and backed out of the dormitory, glancing disapprovingly at Dr. Riggs. He sat under a tree, feeling dismal and helpless, and watched the clouds move across the sky. As he sat there a group of young men arrived from up the river. For all appearances, they were already accomplished young warriors.

Ah, but it was so good for Yesa to see their handsome white, blue, and red blankets and their long hair! Yesa had not worn such a costume since his father had cut his hair and given him an ill-fitting pair of pants and a shirt. Compared to these handsome young braves, he felt like a wild goose whose wings had been clipped.

But he also realized that soon these new boys would be turned into imitation white men. Their hair would be hacked off and their blankets would be taken away. They would learn to read the prayers in the book and they would be given strange new names. Yesa shook his head in dismay as he sat under the cottonwoods and pondered these sad thoughts.

Moments later, he was roused from his meditation when the Mandan boy he had seen in the chapel came out of the dormitory looking as unhappy and confused as Yesa. After looking around the grounds with one sweeping glance, he sat down next to Yesa and the two young men looked at each other in silence. They stayed there in the shade of the big tree for a very long time. Finally Yesa whispered in English, "And what has Doctor Riggs done to your name? Did he steal it as he stole mine?"

The Mandan did not speak. He shook his head with deep regret, but he did not utter a word. He understood English, but he was too miserable to reply.

"Ai . . ." Yesa murmured with great distress. "What is to become of us if we give up everything we have been? How will we ever find our way into this new world of white men?"

Again the two young men were silent. Then the Mandan muttered, "*Alfred* . . . that is the name he gave me. *Alfred Mandan!*"

Before Yesa could respond, they heard the voice of a young girl. She was standing with her parents and Dr. Riggs near the Dakota Home for Girls. As her parents began to leave, the young woman broke free of the doctor's grasp and ran screaming into her mother's arms.

"I cannot do it! I cannot stay here! I will die, Mother! I will die! Don't make me stay here with them!"

The parents embraced the girl and tried to reason with her, but she continued to cry hysterically.

The two young men watched in silent misery as her parents led the girl back to the Dakota Home in spite of her pleadings. The scene outraged them, and it was all they could do not to spring to their feet and try to aid the helpless girl.

"We can do nothing," the Mandan muttered between his teeth. "We can do nothing to help ourselves and we can do nothing to help her!"

But Yesa shook his head. "Yes, there is something we can do," he said with great determination. "We can learn so much that we can outsmart them! We can become so wise in their own knowledge that we can rise above them. We can teach our people everything we learn, until we are no longer strangers in our own land! We can do all of this so we can learn, to survive! And then how proud we will be to have kept our grandmothers alive within us! That is what we can do!"

It was this angry determination that helped Alexander East and Alfred Mandan to excel in their studies. They thought of nothing but succeeding, and they both worked harder than they had ever worked in their lives. They needed no encouragement from their teachers. They needed no inspiration or praise. They were not afraid of the books that had once terrified them with their unintelligible words, and they were not afraid of work.

"The white man has no use for Indians," Alfred confided to his friend. "I have read in the newspaper that Sitting Bull and the northern Cheyennes are fighting in Wyoming and Montana. So how will we manage to continue our studies when the whites want only to defeat us?"

"It will happen," Alexander insisted. "Believe what I am telling you, Alfred. If we are their best pupils they will have to recognize our abilities. They will have to send us to college!"

It was a dream, but both young men believed in it utterly and devoted every hour to its realization. They took turns sawing firewood for the instructors and their wives, and before long they had some money of their own. At night they counted their earnings and hid them away. This would be the money that would take them East to a university.

When they were not sawing wood and doing odd jobs for Dr. Riggs, they studied harder than any of the other students. Soon they had completely mastered English. By the end of their second year they could translate every word of their English primer into their native languages. They had caught up with students who had started school two and three years before they had, and were already studying elementary algebra and geometry.

When they were called upon to answer questions in class, they did not hesitate. The days when Alexander would cringe if a teacher called upon him to answer a question were far behind him. There was no timidity left in his behavior. Even his rage had changed into an almost fatalistic determination. The future had become something tangible and real, something he could almost see, something he could reach out and touch! It no longer mattered by what name people called him. It didn't matter what clothes he wore, or what language he spoke. He had kept alive within him the most important lessons of his people. The impact of the white man's knowledge had not caused them to fade. Instead, his silent belief in them had increased. He had learned how to use his intelligence to fortify his heritage and to see in the generations of his people a power and reality that he had never before been able to see.

Then one day Dr. Riggs sent for Alexander and Alfred and told them that he had arranged to send both of them to Beloit, Wisconsin, where they would enter the preparatory department of Beloit College.

Alexander smiled with a joy so vast that it almost brought tears to his eyes. He and Alfred looked at each other with excitement, hearts bursting with pleasure. This was the great opportunity for which they had been striving for two years!

It was the most jubilant time of their lives, and they celebrated the enormous victory with boundless energy, while the other students looked on in amazement. Alexander and Alfred had been so determined, industrious, and serious, that now their fellow classmates were shocked by their unbridled revelry.

\* \* \*

Then came the news, on what was to have been the eve of their departure, that Alexander's father had died in Flandreau after only two days' illness.

Alexander trembled when Dr. Riggs told him the news. He felt as if his whole life was collapsing inside of him. It was in obedience to his father that he had set out on this insane venture. It was for this tireless father that he had given up everything he loved to become something new and strange!

Alfred stayed with Alexander and tried to comfort him, but it took a long time for the immensity of Alexander's ambition to overtake his feelings of melancholy and grief. Finally, after many weeks, it was clear to him that the father who had sought him among the tribes and set him on a new trail should be obeyed to the end. He, Alexander East, would serve his father and his tribe.

He did not go back to Flandreau. Instead, in September of 1876 he left Dr. Riggs's mission school with his friend Alfred and journeyed to Beloit to begin his life again.

# Part Six

# In Search of
# the Real

# PHARISEES

The long journey to Beloit College was filled with difficult adjustments. Alexander and Alfred might have been considered accomplished young men among their own people, but in this strange new world they were utter children. Alexander had some advantage, for he had known a few whites at the trading posts and had spent a year with his father in Flandreau. As awed and fearful as he was at every turn, he was calm in comparison to Alfred, who had lived entirely secluded among the Mandan Indians until arriving at Dr. Riggs's mission school.

"Ah!" murmured Alfred in dread, when they arrived at Yankton City's railroad station. "What is that?"

Alexander tried to comfort his friend as they boarded the train, but Alfred would not set foot on the monster until he had made a cautious inspection of the huge locomotive.

"It is going to be all right," Alexander kept whispering, as he tugged at Alfred's sleeve and pulled him aboard the restless, steaming dragon. "I was scared out of my wits the first time I was on one of these trains," he admitted. "But it is only a machine, Alfred . . . nothing to be frightened of, believe me."

His friend nodded dubiously and carefully took his place next to Alexander on the soft, green velvet seat. Moments later, the train began to rumble, and then they were off!

Every hour and every turn brought a new discovery—a whirling succession of visions that passed like the blurred telegraph poles which sped past the windows as the train hurtled into the unknown.

Though Alfred was finally relaxed and even enjoying his first train ride, Alexander was deeply troubled. They were moving farther and farther away from the vast, open land of Indians. More and more they were entering a region so crowded with houses and fields and barns that it seemed far too small for the inhabitants. The towns and villages that flashed past the windows of the train were growing larger and larger and closer together, until at last there was no land. There was no earth. And finally, the train reached an enormous, smoky city where it was necessary to change trains, a matter that Dr. Riggs had prearranged with the conductors. But despite the conductors' assistance, the crowds and bustle and billowing steam gave the two young men a terrible fright.

The noise! The air seemed to burst with commotion. The streets were so crowded with people that Alexander could not imagine why they did not continually bump into each other. And the rushing! Everybody seemed to be in the greatest possible hurry, as if they were under attack. The constant noise and the sight of all the bustling people greatly alarmed Alfred, and it was all Alexander could do to contain his own anxiety, in order to calm his fearful friend.

"They are just crazy," Alexander whispered. "Pay no attention to them. They are the children of ants. That is what they remind me of—ants!"

This cheered Alfred a bit, and he forgot about the chaos of the streets as he began to realize that all the passers-by were staring at them.

"Why are they looking at us?" he asked.

Alexander laughed self-consciously and said, "Don't pay any attention to them. Just act as though we are a couple of princes from Arabia! Just hold up your head and look straight ahead!"

"But—"

"Do as I say, Alfred. . . . Don't let them intimidate you! After all, we are going to Beloit College!"

The conductor pointed the two friends to an eating house, accompanying them to the door. He left them with a very pretty waitress, whose bright blue eyes and breathlessly rapid speech were at once intoxicating and alarming.

Since he couldn't understand her jumbled speech, Alexander thought it best that he and Alfred agree with every suggestion the waitress made. He nodded politely, no matter what she said, and before long the girl had brought them almost everything that was listed on the menu. Staring wide-eyed at the food piled on the table in front of them, Alexander and Alfred grew very worried. It was clear that they did not have enough money to pay for it all. Just as they were about to panic, the conductor walked in and angrily chastised the waitress for playing such a cruel prank.

"They look like a couple of Injuns to me. . . ." she said, and shrugged as the customers began to laugh. "How'm I supposed to know what a couple of heathens want for lunch?" The restaurant was suddenly filled with such loud laughter that the conductor immediately led his embarrassed young wards into the street.

"Never you mind," he muttered, trying to cheer Alexander and Alfred. "We'll get something for you to eat on the train. We've got to hurry up if you're going to get seats."

When they finally reached Beloit on the second day of their pilgrimage, they discovered a city that was beautifully located on the high, wooded banks of the stately Rock River. The college grounds covered the site of an ancient village that had been peopled by Indian mound-builders. These Indians had made hundreds of large ceremonial pyramids of soil before completely vanishing, leaving no trace of their civilization except the sprawling mounds.

Alexander and Alfred were taken to the house of the college president, Dr. Chapin, and after a brief polite greeting, the boys were shown to their room in South College. Alexander blew a sigh of relief and immediately threw open all the windows to let in the wind and smell of grass.

For a moment Alexander gazed out the window with deep happiness and a marvelous sense of fulfillment. Here he was at last—at a college where only the best white students were accepted, in a fine, clean room with his friend Alfred Mandan, in an alien and remote galaxy where few Indians had ever ventured! But then his happy mood abruptly changed, for in the wind he heard a young man shouting across the Common: "Hurry up, Turkey, or you'll not have a chance to see him! We have Sitting Bull's nephew right here! And it's more than likely he'll have your scalplock before morning!"

It was September of 1876—just three months since General Custer and his command had been defeated. White people were extremely bitter, and the Beloit newspaper, learning that two Indian boys had won scholarships to the college, had printed a story claiming that Alexander East was the nephew of Sitting Bull.

In a moment the boy called "Turkey," the son of a missionary, pranced up to the window and stared unabashedly at Alexander and Alfred.

"Which one of you guys is the nephew?" he flatly asked.

Alexander slammed the window closed.

"Let's just forget about it," he told Alfred, who was ready to run outside and thrash Turkey. "Let's just try to overlook it. Do you hear? They don't even know what they're saying! Half of them have never even seen an Indian before. So let's just try to forget about it."

It was not an easy matter to ignore the insults and teasing. When Alexander and Alfred went into town they were followed on the streets by gangs of little white savages who gave imitation war whoops. Even the adults smirked with undisguised disdain as they stared at the two friends.

"It simply doesn't matter what they think," Alexander repeated again and again. "We have been invited here because we are fine students, and as long as we do our work and mind our own business, they cannot ask us to leave."

"But we are not wanted here," Alfred said sadly.

"We also are not wanted at home. We are just going to have to make a place for ourselves. There is no other way. . . . We have come too far to turn back now. I don't know exactly where we are going, Alfred, but we have to *keep* going, because there is no where else for us."

Alexander's first major recitation at Beloit was a big event in his life. He was brought before a remarkable-looking man whose name was Professor Pettibone. He had a long, grave face with very long whiskers, scarcely any hair on his head, and a decided stammer that kept time with his continually blinking little eyes. He seemed more like a rabbit than a person, and yet he was the very embodiment of wisdom; he was surely the best instructor at Beloit.

Unlike at his previous school, Alexander was very nervous when asked to recite or to demonstrate mathematical problems. His written lessons did not worry him, but he became shy and withdrawn when asked to answer questions aloud. Suddenly his command of English seemed to vanish and he would stammer and bite his lip, feeling completely mortified.

"What . . . what's this!" Professor Pettibone now exclaimed, thinking that Alexander's stammering was an imitation of his own speech impediment.

"I am deeply sorry, sir," Alexander said quietly, "b-b-but I have a pro-problem about sp-sp-speaking English. It is difficult f-f-for me to recite my lessons, sir."

A fond smile gradually formed on Professor Pettibone's grave face. He nodded his head with deep sympathy and gave Alexander a reassuring pat on the shoulder. "Well, then," he stammered, "y-y-you and—I have so-so-something in common, my boy. But I-I-I've never let it s-s-stop me . . . an-an-and neither sh-sh-should you!"

Alexander heaved a sigh of relief and laughed happily while Professor Pettibone gave him a warm handshake. At last he could begin to feel confident about his lessons, because he knew that somebody believed in him.

Soon he was able to speak fluently in front of a whole room of students. He absorbed knowledge through his pores. The more he learned, the greater his capacity for learning became. He wanted to know everything about the world, because everything he learned taught him something about himself. And the more he understood about himself, the stronger he felt about the special mission he had chosen for his life: to use the white man's wisdom to keep his Indian heritage alive.

And yet, Alexander found it difficult to trust anyone. He never entirely understood what white people were feeling inside. *They are such curious animals,* he would think to himself. *They turn everything around from the way it is among Indians. They believe it is a person's duty to tell the truth, and are always talking about the importance of truth. Yet they never express their thoughts honestly. They*

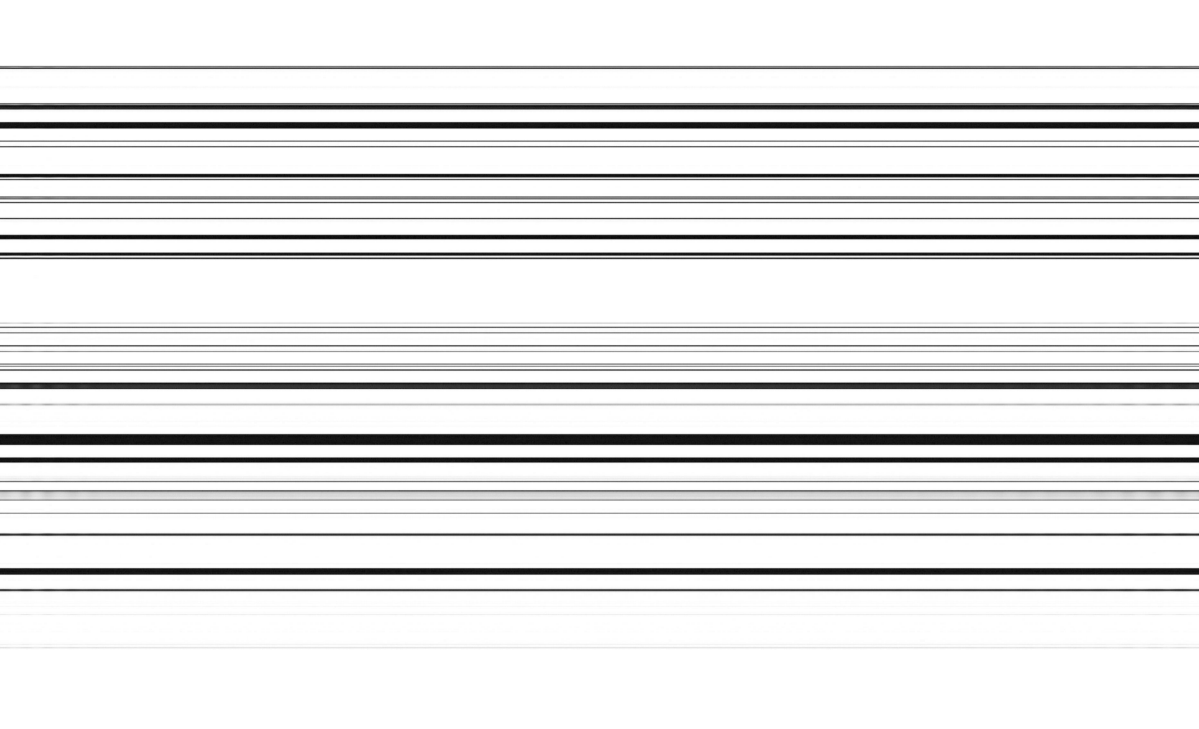

s and their fathers'
w much money they
truthful about what
bout it, the more
hful about all the

lexander decided
are mu-mu-much
k-keeping them!"
cher.
t-t-teach us w-w-
s-should be y-y-

in Professor Petti-
with incidents of
soon recovered
a great chasm—
ination than ever.
ult at Beloit. The
and skepticism of
courage. He was
one as his proctor,
anger. He began
low in understand-
the other students,
a sense of failure

e's help on behalf
o, but the Profes-
problems that con-
difficult for Alfred
at our anticipations

of this new life were all w r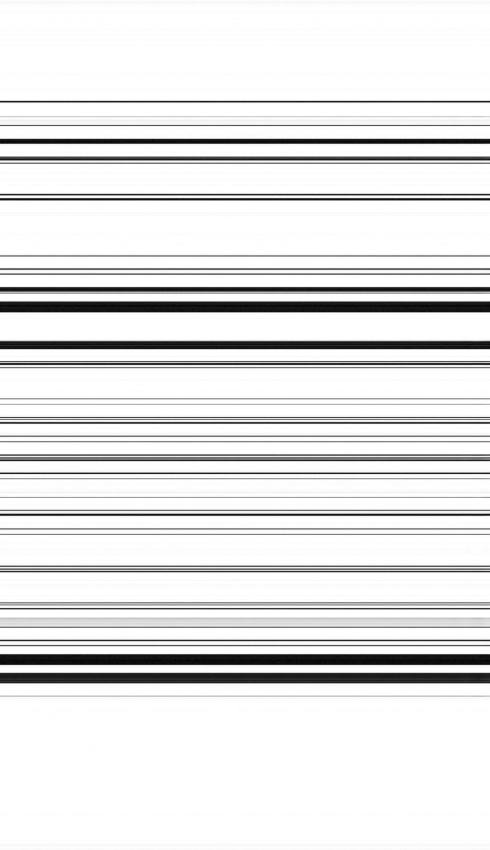
lems entirely new to us. It i
us to learn. We are both g
hard at lessons. But there is
us to learn.''
   Professor Pettibone stro k
The expression of sympath y
ander to speak openly.
   ''I wish you could help
behind, and if he is asked t
continue all by myself.'' Ale
and sat looking at his han d
searching for.
   ''Alfred is smart,'' he sai d
a lake or to run with a m e
country, he could do thes e
understand how to go abou t
things we are asked to do h
us. It is only recently that I
man's idea that each word h
name. It is only now that I g r
all these many words, stan d
words, like the bricks in a
   ''Yes. . . .'' Professor P e t
   ''I have come to realiz e
words, but to Alfred these s
surround him with walls h e
   For a long time the teach e
in silence. Alexander waite d
him through this most com p
to face since leaving the lan d
clear that the wise and goo d
the prison of words that su r

run outside and thrash Turkey. "Let's just try to overlook it. Do you hear? They don't even know what they're saying! Half of them have never even seen an Indian before. So let's just try to forget about it."

It was not an easy matter to ignore the insults and teasing. When Alexander and Alfred went into town they were followed on the streets by gangs of little white savages who gave imitation war whoops. Even the adults smirked with undisguised disdain as they stared at the two friends.

"It simply doesn't matter what they think," Alexander repeated again and again. "We have been invited here because we are fine students, and as long as we do our work and mind our own business, they cannot ask us to leave."

"But we are not wanted here," Alfred said sadly.

"We also are not wanted at home. We are just going to have to make a place for ourselves. There is no other way. . . . We have come too far to turn back now. I don't know exactly where we are going, Alfred, but we have to *keep* going, because there is no where else for us."

Alexander's first major recitation at Beloit was a big event in his life. He was brought before a remarkable-looking man whose name was Professor Pettibone. He had a long, grave face with very long whiskers, scarcely any hair on his head, and a decided stammer that kept time with his continually blinking little eyes. He seemed more like a rabbit than a person, and yet he was the very embodiment of wisdom; he was surely the best instructor at Beloit.

Unlike at his previous school, Alexander was very nervous when asked to recite or to demonstrate mathematical problems. His written lessons did not worry him, but he became shy and withdrawn when asked to answer questions aloud. Suddenly his command of English seemed to vanish and he would stammer and bite his lip, feeling completely mortified.

"What . . . what's this!" Professor Pettibone now exclaimed, thinking that Alexander's stammering was an imitation of his own speech impediment.

"I am deeply sorry, sir," Alexander said quietly, "b-b-but I have a pro-problem about sp-sp-speaking English. It is difficult f-f-for me to recite my lessons, sir."

A fond smile gradually formed on Professor Pettibone's grave face. He nodded his head with deep sympathy and gave Alexander a reassuring pat on the shoulder. "Well, then," he stammered, "y-y-you and—I have so-so-something in common, my boy. But I-I-I've never let it s-s-stop me . . . an-an-and neither sh-sh-should you!"

Alexander heaved a sigh of relief and laughed happily while Professor Pettibone gave him a warm handshake. At last he could begin to feel confident about his lessons, because he knew that somebody believed in him.

Soon he was able to speak fluently in front of a whole room of students. He absorbed knowledge through his pores. The more he learned, the greater his capacity for learning became. He wanted to know everything about the world, because everything he learned taught him something about himself. And the more he understood about himself, the stronger he felt about the special mission he had chosen for his life: to use the white man's wisdom to keep his Indian heritage alive.

And yet, Alexander found it difficult to trust anyone. He never entirely understood what white people were feeling inside. *They are such curious animals,* he would think to himself. *They turn everything around from the way it is among Indians. They believe it is a person's duty to tell the truth, and are always talking about the importance of truth. Yet they never express their thoughts honestly. They*

*freely tell all kinds of personal details—their names and their fathers'
names, the dates and places of their births, even how much money they
have in their pockets—but they are unwilling to be truthful about what
they believe in.* The more Alexander thought about it, the more
it seemed to him that white people were truthful about all the
wrong things.

"Well . . ." Professor Pettibone said, when Alexander decided
to share these thoughts. "It's true that w-w-we are mu-mu-much
better at ma-ma-making rules than we are at k-k-keeping them!"

Alexander grinned affectionately at his teacher.

"Wh-what you mu-mu-must do, my boy, is t-t-teach us w-w-
what we are t-t-trying to teach y-y-you. That s-s-should be y-y-
your mission in life!"

Alexander instantly recognized the wisdom in Professor Pettibone's comment. Though his days were filled with incidents of
subtle ridicule and embarrassing moments, he soon recovered
his balance—like a brave walking a ledge over a great chasm—
and set to work on his studies with more determination than ever.

Alfred, however, was finding life very difficult at Beloit. The
cruelties of the students and the indifference and skepticism of
the instructors broke down his ambition and courage. He was
not fortunate enough to have Professor Pettibone as his proctor,
and he gradually became lost in melancholy and anger. He began
to stumble in his studies. At first he was just slow in understanding, but as he fell further and further behind the other students,
he became so overwhelmed by depression and a sense of failure
that he had no hope of ever catching up.

Alexander tried to enlist Professor Pettibone's help on behalf
of Alfred. Alexander found college difficult too, but the Professor always managed to pull him through the problems that confused him. "One of the reasons school is so difficult for Alfred
and me," he told the professor one day, "is that our anticipations

of this new life were all wrong. We are confronted with problems entirely new to us. It is more than just the lessons you ask us to learn. We are both good students and are willing to work hard at lessons. But there is something more difficult that you ask us to learn."

Professor Pettibone stroked his beard and listened carefully. The expression of sympathy in his gentle eyes encouraged Alexander to speak openly.

"I wish you could help Alfred, Professor. He is falling far behind, and if he is asked to leave school I do not know if I can continue all by myself." Alexander stopped talking for a moment and sat looking at his hands, trying to find the words he was searching for.

"Alfred is smart," he said finally. "If he was told to swim across a lake or to run with a message through a wild and unknown country, he could do these things quickly and well. He would understand how to go about doing what you ask of him. But the things we are asked to do here at Beloit are strange and new to us. It is only recently that I have begun to understand the white man's idea that each word has a place and a power and a specific name. It is only now that I grasp the concept that all these words, all these many words, stand in some kind of relation to all other words, like the bricks in a wall."

"Yes. . . ." Professor Pettibone said softly.

"I have come to realize that I can build things with these words, but to Alfred these same words have become bricks that surround him with walls he cannot escape."

For a long time the teacher and student looked at each other in silence. Alexander waited anxiously for his professor to help him through this most complicated of all problems he had had to face since leaving the land of his people. Gradually it became clear that the wise and good Professor Pettibone could not see the prison of words that surrounded the world.

Alexander looked away sadly. Then he remembered the words of a wise man:

> *For those who are walled up,*
> *everything is a wall*
> *. . . even an open door.*

By summer vacation Alfred Mandan had been released from school and Alexander found himself alone.

When the next school year began, some of the students were genial and spoke to him after classes, but no one invited him to the parties and athletic events that were popular among the young people.

A few of the boys came from poor families and so had to earn money for at least part of their college expenses. These students were by far the most friendly to Alexander, as well as the most diligent students. But they too, for the most part, remained remote and impersonal during the three years that Alexander studied at Beloit College.

In truth, however, he had little time to socialize. Since he had no money of his own, and the Government had not made provision for an Indian to get an education, Alexander had to go out in search of work. On Saturdays he usually sawed wood and did chores for some of the professors.

When winter descended he missed Alfred more than ever, feeling lonelier than he had in a long time. He sat in his empty room, staring at the bed where his friend had slept, thinking about Uncheedah and Mysterious Medicine. He wondered if they were sitting in their warm lodge somewhere on the great wide plains of Canada, free and happy. And he thought of beautiful Oesedah and her lovely little face and her shy glances. And his heart grew frantic for her.

How he longed to have news of his family! But they could not understand written words, and so it would do no good to write them letters. There was no way he could reach out to them. How he longed to be with Oesedah! How he wanted to hear the voice of his grandmother and the jokes of Matogee and the solemn lectures of Mysterious Medicine!

He whispered each of their names in the night and waited anxiously for the wind to answer. But the wind in Wisconsin was a prisoner of walls, too, and could not escape the buildings and crowded streets to blow free and full across the open land. The cities had turned the long-whispering voice of the Great Mystery into a frozen gale that chilled everything it touched. And the wind said nothing. It was a wind without a voice. Even if you listened for many hours, it told you nothing.

The next summer Alexander decided to hire himself out as a farm helper, and after requesting and receiving a letter of introduction from the college president, he set out in search of work. As he walked toward the outskirts of the city and into the farmlands that surrounded Beloit, he searched for traces of animals. He studied the road for their tracks and he listened carefully for their calls. But there were no animals and there were no sounds, except the occasional grunt of a cow corraled in a muddy little pen, where it stood placidly without expression or dignity. An animal without a soul. Another prisoner of the walls.

The sight of these fat, stupid beasts angered Alexander, for he could recall the sleek, swift animals who ran among the trees. And as he shuffled down the road toward a farmhouse hidden among the tall stalks of corn, he recalled the battles of the great chief Black Hawk of the Sauk and Fox tribe, who had fought to keep this very region free less than forty-six years earlier. Now there was no trace of that desperate struggle. The Indians were gone. Black Hawk was gone. And all that remained was the silent cry of a defeated people that rose from the soil and brought a great melancholy to Alexander East.

He approached the front door of the farmhouse with misgivings. A young woman peeked out at him and asked him to wait. He could read in her clear blue eyes the thoughts that were passing through her mind. She was afraid of him.

He waited for a very long time, and finally saw out of the corners of his eyes the farmer come in from the field and enter his home by another door, apparently taking great precautions.

"Well," he said, when he poked his head out the door. "What is it you want?"

"I am a student of Beloit College, sir, but the college is closed for the summer and I am looking for work."

"Uh-huh . . ." he muttered, looking Alexander up and down with a mixture of astonishment and alarm. "You're some kind of Injun, ain't you?"

"Yes, sir."

"Well, that settles it. You're not going to massacre anybody 'round here, so just get off my property quick as you can! I got a cousin killed by you people only last summer! So you jest get before I put a couple of holes in your head!"

Alexander backed away with a calm dignity that had become second nature to him now. No matter how much people hurt him, he was armed against their insults. Though he tried to retain the humility that Uncheedah had taught him, it was difficult for him not to realize that he was superior to people who treated him as inferior.

"Good day," he said politely to the farmer.

The dignity in Alexander's manner and the eloquence of his impeccable English brought a surge of rage into the man's coarse face.

"You're nothing but a damn Injun!" he shouted and shook his fist.

"Yes, you are right. That is *exactly* what I am," Alexander said, and turned and slowly walked away.

# MANHOOD

"It may be," Dr. Riggs was saying as he examined Alexander's appearance both through and over his thick glasses, "that your great success in college was due to the very fact that you had so few friends."

Alexander smiled politely but did not respond.

"And, after all," the doctor continued in his terse, paternal tone, "in my experience it is a lack of friendliness that makes a friendless man."

Again Alexander did not answer.

"But in any event," Dr. Riggs went on, puffing a large cigar and brushing the ashes from his voluptuous beard, "you have succeeded, and you have only yourself to thank for your achievements. When you went to Beloit you were one of the first of your race to attend a college. Now there are many!"

"Yes, there are many," Alexander said quietly.

"But you were one of the first! And I must congratulate you, my boy," he exclaimed with a great chuckle of pleasure. "Do you recall when you first came to me? A child barely able to speak. Ah, I remember it very well. But now—look at you! A man! A regular gentleman and a physician besides!"

Alexander was indeed a gentleman and a doctor. He had finished all that he could accomplish at Beloit, and one day

Professor Pettibone had suggested that he go on to an Eastern school and leave Wisconsin behind him. "It's t-t-time, my boy. Yes indeed, it-it-it's time to move on!"

And so he had gone to Dartmouth College, way up among the gray granite hills.

The New England Indians, for whom the college was founded, had come and gone nearly a century earlier. When Alexander East found his way to this stately campus, he became its only Indian student. Though poor, he was able to manage because the college took care of his tuition and expenses under its original charter, which had been devoted to Indian education. And when he was graduated by Dartmouth, a scholarship made it possible for him to study medicine at Boston University.

Now at last school days were over, and Alexander had achieved the goals his father had envisioned for him. But he was no longer certain what his achievements really meant. He had learned much, but he had also lost much. After Alfred Mandan left Beloit College that summer many years ago, Alexander had never made another friend. He simply passed through crowded rooms. He said polite hellos to strangers. He knew people's names, but he knew nothing else about them. He could not get near anyone without some fool making a joke about Indians. It was as if he would never cease being a curiosity.

"And now . . ." Dr. Riggs was asking, munching on his cigar and nodding incessantly. "And now what? Where does the young Indian doctor expect to find his fortune?"

"Excuse me?" Alexander stammered, coming out of a daydream.

"I said . . . where will you be setting up a practice?"

"I am leaving for the reservation tomorrow morning," Alexander said softly. "But I could not pass so close to Santee without coming to see you, Dr. Riggs."

"Then you have forgiven me for giving you a Christian name and making you into a decent God-fearing young man?" the doctor said with a wide smile.

For a moment Alexander gazed distressfully at the old man, and then he said: "I came here to show you what I have become."

"And very proud I am of you!" Dr. Riggs exclaimed, getting up and clasping Alexander by the hand. "Just look at you now! So elegant and polite! Dressed with such style! You will be very hard pressed, my dear boy, to convince some of those Indians up on the reservation that you are still one of them!"

Alexander smiled politely but he did not speak.

Dr. Riggs sensed a chill in the conversation and cleared his throat self-consciously. "Well, what will you do with yourself up there in the wilds?"

"I am going to take charge of the medical work of the reservation."

"Ah," sighed Dr. Riggs, ". . . now *that* is truly noble. I must tell you I am deeply touched by your Christian decision. Most young men of your race who have worked as hard as you for an education would be glad to stay away from the reservation."

Dr. Riggs intended to continue to praise Alexander, but in the middle of his speech he realized that his visitor was already collecting his hat and waiting for a polite moment to say goodbye.

"My dear boy," Dr. Riggs intoned earnestly. "I do hope I have not said something that—"

"Not at all," Alexander said politely, shaking the doctor's hand and backing away.

"Well, it's been a great pleasure and a great honor . . . your coming to see me and all," Dr. Riggs was saying as Alexander withdrew slowly from the room. "There aren't very many of my boys who come back to see me. And I consider myself very lucky indeed to have helped produce such a fine-looking, bright young doctor!''

Alexander pulled the door closed behind him and shuddered for a moment before he looked out into the cool November sky and started down the street.

Part Seven

# The Darkness
# in Men's Eyes

# GHOST DANCE

In the evening Dr. Alexander East stood at his window, gazing toward the place called Wounded Knee, trying to put to rest the ghosts of his people. But nothing could send away the phantoms.

It was dusk when a single, long line of soldiers appeared on the horizon. It was the Seventh Cavalry returning to the reservation with the bodies of its twenty-five dead and thirty-four wounded. The whites of the agency sent up a howl of indignation and anger when they saw the broken bodies of the soldiers. Their rage only increased when they learned that most of the wounds and fatalities were caused by soldiers who had encircled the unarmed Indians and shot anything that moved, including their own comrades.

Soon after the cavalry arrived, it was clear there was not enough room in the dispensary and hospital for the wounded. Father Jutz offered the use of the mission chapel, and the bleeding soldiers were quickly brought in and laid down on the floor under the shadow of the Christmas tree.

With a burst of determination, Alexander helped to tear out the pews where the Indians had prayed, and to cover the floor with hay and quilts. Soon there were row upon row of terribly mutilated young bodies lying side by side. He devoted the entire night to the care of soldiers who had murdered his unarmed people. But they were so pitiable that he could not hate them. They cried out, and they moaned and thrashed their bloody arms, and then they died. By morning most of them were covered with blankets and were carried slowly away to be buried in the new snow, which was now heavily falling.

Alexander could no longer feel or think. He was so weary and so desperately tormented by the terrible waste of life that he could do nothing but stand by the window and watch the endless snow that fell upon the ground. The blizzard lasted the entire day. And in its very midst General Brooke ordered Dr. East and several Indian policemen to search for members of the Indian police who had been reported wounded and missing some distance from the agency.

"Must we go?" a young Indian whispered to Alexander, as he pulled on his heavy coat.

He did not answer. He could not speak. He simply turned to the door and stepped out into the snow and the freezing wind, straining with all his strength to walk to the corral where his horse was waiting. Then he and his party started their search.

They did not find the missing men. The snow was too deep and the wind was so powerful that they could not search the creek bottom where the Indians had disappeared.

Rather than turn back, Alexander insisted that the searchers camp in the shelter of the cottonwoods and continue their efforts to find the missing men the next day.

In the morning the sky cleared, but the ground was entirely covered with fresh snow. Alexander feared that some of the Indians of Big Foot's band might have been left wounded on the battlefield of Wounded Knee. A number of the policemen volunteered to help search for them, while the others returned to the agency to request additional volunteers and wagons in which to carry anyone who might be found alive back to the dispensary.

The day was bright and clear. And the beauty of the sunlit landscape made it impossible for Alexander to comprehend the dreadful slaughter that had taken place at Wounded Knee. Fully three miles from the scene of the massacre they found the first battered body: a woman buried in the snow, her child still clinging to her. That was only the first of hundreds of corpses. From that point on the police began to find twisted, frozen bodies, lying with wide eyes, arms thrown forward, and mouths held open in a silent scream. The victims had been shot down as they fled, crying for their lives.

The wailing began as the volunteers found friends and relatives among the great heaps of the dead, and there was such mourning and weeping that the hills sank to their knees, and the Sun, mad with grief, covered his face and left the world in darkness.

When the searchers reached the place where the Indian camp had stood, they found burned and battered lodges and snow stained with trails of blood. Bodies were everywhere, piled one upon another.

Alexander stopped and knelt in the snow by the figure of a child. Her arm had been blown off. Her frozen hair spread into jagged points like an outcry. And in her little eyes there was a look of such vast and unending agony that Alexander could not move or gesture or speak.

Everywhere the searchers were singing death songs as they came upon the broken bodies of friends. The sound roused Alexander from his fearful dream, and he staggered to his feet. Stumbling among the corpses of his people, he wept at the unspeakable devastation of the camp.

Under a splintered wagon Alexander found an old woman, blind and whimpering. She had crawled away and hidden under the wagon until the fighting had ceased. Then she had listened to the dying people begging for help as the soldiers trudged among the bodies, shooting anyone who was still alive. At last it was quiet, and the old woman had prayed as the blizzard fell upon the valley, covering the bloody limbs of her relatives, freezing them into grotesque statues.

Now the old woman touched Alexander's face with trembling fingers as she tried to thank him for saving her.

Silently the wagons loaded with the few survivors were dispatched for the agency, and Alexander followed the wretched caravan on his own horse.

In the snow the women moved to and fro, shaking their heads and beating their breasts. The sunlight would not return; thick clouds slowly covered the terrible valley. Blood flowed in the rivers, and the sky was dark and starless and blind.

Surely now the sacred tree was dead, and spring would never come again to Indian people.

In the evening Alexander still stood at his window, gazing toward the place called Wounded Knee, trying to put to rest the ghosts and the corpses, the frozen fingers, and the fear-filled eyes that haunted him. But absolutely nothing was able to send away these terrible phantoms until, suddenly, a small red bird fluttered against the windowpane, chirping and shaking its feathers in a magical dance.

Alexander sighed as he peered at the creature, holding his breath and carefully moving toward the little red bird. Hesitantly, he made a tiny sound like the one he had made as a boy when he talked with the animals.

For just a moment the bird understood him. Momentarily it hovered close and looked through the window at Alexander, blinking its mysterious, fiery eyes, in which there was something immense and unexplainable. Then it burst into flight.

For a very long time Alexander looked out, watching the tiny red bird flit aimlessly in the blind, dark sky.

Alexander turned around and around in the darkness, trying to find the center. He was filled with fragile memories, with songs and prayers and phantoms of people.

"I was mistaken," the voice of Yesa was saying to him. "I was mistaken."

# STORY'S END

The great island seas of northern Minnesota and the Province of Ontario are surrounded by impenetrable forests. The immense unyielding bogs called *muskegs* are filled with tamaracks, and the higher land with white pines, cedars, poplars, and deep groves of white birch. The land is a paradise where moose and deer lumber free and glistening black waters wind their way through endless reaches of unbroken silence. There are blueberries and cranberries in abundance, and in the inland bays tall acres of wild rice undulate in the slightest breeze.

In this world of freedom and plenty a few Indians still live isolated and happy, almost unconscious of the bare pathos of their survival. Here the early French traders bartered for furs and then settled and married among the natives. They brought nothing with them. What they received was a rich, long-resounding heritage of the Indians who welcomed them into their families. The dense labyrinth of mire and bogs has protected them from the encroachment of strangers far more effectually than treaties. It was to this singular paradise that Yesa, leaving Alexander East behind, went in search of himself and of the center where the sacred tree still grows.